DANCELAND

DANCELAND

a novella

Jennifer Pieroni 4/28/14

For Kim,

Much Love,

Jen

Queen's Ferry Press

Queen's Ferry Press
8622 Naomi Street
Plano, TX 75024
www.queensferrypress.com

Published 2014 by Queen's Ferry Press

Cover design by Adam Pieroni

First edition March 2014

ISBN 978-1-938466-20-5

Printed in the United States of America

Praise for DANCELAND:

"Finding the perfect balance between language and story, Jennifer Pieroni guides the reader through the twists and turns of the lives of misfit daughter-father duo, Lettie and Frank, and of Lynn, the impetus for their cloistered lives. The deep tentacles of addiction and co-dependency, of fear and redemption, run thick through the forest of this tale of learning to let go of those who hold you captive with their fear and disease. With love, Pieroni teaches us that no matter how much we want to protect that which we hold most dear, the world is out there waiting to terrorize us, to envelop us, to enchant us, and to teach us how to accept, if not fully forgive. Read this book, dear reader, and fall hopelessly in love, the way I have, with *Danceland*."

—Myfanwy Collins, author of *Echolocation* and *I Am Holding Your Hand*

"Jennifer Pieroni is a born writer with the ear of a poet and the eye of a mother hawk. In her first novella, she's created a questioning, reclusive young girl who, left to her own devices, leaves the troubled haven her father has created to go in search of her own life, and the hard truths that are hers to know."

—Pia Z. Ehrhardt, author of *Famous Fathers & Other Stories*

"Jennifer Pieroni has written a novella of careful observation, of intimate insight. This is a work of beauty from a writer and editor who has always known that to sweat the small stuff is to make a story as big as it can be."

—Matthew Salesses, author of *I'm Not Saying, I'm Just Saying* and *The Last Repatriate*

"In her debut novella *Danceland*, Jennifer Pieroni has exquisitely captured an archaic loneliness we often associate with childhood. *Danceland* explores the blurred lines between the beauty of solitude and the deep ache of loneliness with grace and elegance. The emotional stuff of the book is powerful and lingering. It is a gorgeous accomplishment."

—Claudia Smith, author of *Quarry Light*

For Domenic

In Heaven a noble work was done
when God gave man a Mother.

Irish Proverb

Here's what she knew: *Mum was a dancer. Dad was a tree trimmer.*

Lettie never knew her mother. Her father, she knew. His truck climbed the hill early, while the night's sweat still soaked the field. All day the clouds changed shape and passed overhead. Later, a sickle moon poked through the blue sky and he returned. His name was Frank.

He left in the morning, and Lettie stayed home. Her bedroom was up the stairs. Frank's room was down the stairs and down the stairs again. In the middle was the woodstove, cast-iron pans hanging from the brickwork, a sandy rug that the cat, Nosey, convulsed on. Their rickety cottage, its shingles loose, was all that was left of Danceland. They were Danceland's survivors.

Every day she was to do a number of things: haul the stumps from the bed of Frank's truck and keep the woodpile shoulder-high, peel and boil the meal, mend the knees and toes of their garments, and read aloud from the brittle, yellow pages of dog-eared arts journals. Reviews of her mother's performances, stories, instructions for practical living.

Years slipped away.

Until she was twelve, Lettie knew no fear. Then, one day, it came. She lay in bed, the muscles in her abdomen pulsing as if to music, blood from the first day of her curse on the insides of her thighs. Downstairs, Frank's boots thumped from stove to faucet. The kettle became hot and bawled. Drawers opened and closed. The cabinets shut. Front door locked. Lettie knelt by the window and watched Frank sip his tea from a takeaway mug and rev the truck's engine before bouncing over the heaves and shallows of the dirt road out toward the gate.

She grew too fast, her pant cuffs hanging mid-calf, the collar of a fisherman's sweater choking her. Instead of asking again for a change of clothes, she descended the steps, down and down again. On his bureau Frank collected greasy wire and antennae. His room smelled like pennies and aged, cold stone. She slid into a pair of his oldest trousers, the knees soft as her cat's paw. Clothes to run in.

After her breakfast of toast and tea, Lettie opened the porch door to the field. The night before, she'd decided she would follow the first low-flying airplane, wade through the grass in the direction of its white trail. It did not take long for the rush of a plane to fill the atmosphere. She let the porch door creak shut.

Midmorning snakes whispered through the grass and the early insects zipped from one wheaty tip to another. Following the vapor trail brought Lettie to the woods, where it was difficult to see through the treetops. So Lettie followed her intuition. And Nosey accompanied her to a point, but then slowed, lagged behind, whisking her tail, forgetting.

Lettie had spent her childhood here. She knew the brook, the standstill pond green with lily pads, an early burial ground, and a minor collection of pear trees dropping diseased fruit. Now she walked for some time, past the sun's height, before resting in a warm dale.

The previous night, as she'd read aloud to him, her father corrected her. "Revival. Re-vive," he said.

"Re-vive," Lettie repeated. "Revive. Sorry."

"That's okay," Frank said.

She read on before asking, "Why haven't you corrected me

before? I must have read this more than a hundred times, always pronounced wrong."

"Never occurred to me," he said, sipping tea.

"Did you teach me to read?"

"Your mum did."

"I don't remember that," she said.

"And you don't remember Danceland either."

"I know. Remind me why."

"A high fever. Higher than natural. It changed your mind and took away your memory."

Frank was right about Lettie's mind. Some days it was so dense, so pressurized, so filled with a loud nothing. She wished things would come clear, but she knew she was lost when it came to what was real. She wouldn't know *real* if she saw it.

Her mother's name was Carolyn Brody Taylor. Her legs were made of coils. Her arms of slow-flowing sand. And her fingers of the dust that floats in the afternoon. These were things Lettie learned about her mum from reading.

Arabesque. Pirouette. Cambré.

Lettie would have liked to dance, to energetically shake free, but her legs wobbled on the sandy rug. She was as inelegant as the songbird drunk on poison berries, flying into the time-warped glass. No, dancing was not something her mother had taught her, unless the fever took that too.

Any other day she would have turned back: to peel the vegetables, to change into clothes of her own, to care for Nosey quivering on the rug, but that day the force was strong. Lettie was like air behind a cork, pushing on past the burnt-down homes of Danceland, and over the loose foundations. Up the climbs and down the trails. The people living there must have loved her mum.

Her dad was a tree trimmer. He worked the odd job. No one in town knew him personally. He bought donuts from the machine in the airport lobby. He picked trash. His manner was gentle, remorseful. He came and went.

Part One

DREAMING

LETTIE

SECOND TO HER FATHER, Lettie loved her cat Nosey. The cat would rise sneezing from a dust mound, training the thread spool along the baseboard, when suddenly she'd break away, having lost her focus on the prowl and hunt. Her character was broken up; she slept less than usual. She did not mind the snow, as she should, and scratched at the door to be let out.

As Frank prepared his tea Lettie outfitted herself for the weather, wrapping a stretched knit scarf four times around her neck and pulling it over her face so that she could smell skin. Only then did she and her cat emerge into the white world outside.

In winter Frank rarely brought back new trees, except for the occasional down from an ice storm or snow weight. These tree trunks were already sawed into three icy sections, wide as Lettie's hug. She carried them that way, embraced, over the pack and under the tarp. They might not thaw and dry this season, so she kept them in the glistening stack, ready for spring.

She piled the wood as tall as she was according to its tone and texture, such that it resembled a sedimentary record.

Even in the bitter cold, pitch still dripped. The smell of the brown glue on her sleeve and hands always reminded her of living things, living things yet to come. Some mornings she went there just for the leaking scent.

From beside her sculpture, beneath the tarp, their troubled home looked small. Every passing year made it seem smaller—smaller and more troubled. Every new novel Lettie read put into focus how they were living. Books about extended families together in clustered houses, friendships made stronger through shared adventure, the endless potential of the individual. Yet, there she was in the dark and crooked shingled shack with only her father. No lines, not for heat, not for toilet. Danceland. What was left of Danceland.

The front door closed. Frank's narrow and apologetic face also betrayed him, a frown sticking out of a plaid overcoat. He looked like a very sorry man indeed as he waved goodbye for the day.

She began to notice: some days the truck turned left, some days right. Some days the truck traveled straight. Every trail eventually died, became obscured by overgrowth. She wasn't looking hard enough. She was hardly looking. Every day, he left. Every day, she stayed. This was the pattern of their lives, the texture, the lonely and fruitless and familiar cycle that had spanned years.

The dried wood was stacked neatly beneath another tarp on the sun-drenched back porch. She'd read that classical ballet relied on something called *muscle memory*. She wondered if splitting did too. How hard it was, in the beginning, for the ax to find the wood. Frank's method was to curve back and drop chop. Frank had dressed her blisters with Band-Aids and ointment. He'd told her how important lumber was to them. His livelihood, he said. What made their meat suitable for eating, kept their blood warm under their skin. Said his confidence in her was not a question. And soon enough, she could split with poise, even took pleasure in the interruption it provided, and in her father's pride. Years passed. Splitting came to feel like everything else.

Supper, she drank tea by the porch door and studied a journal about food. Stories, essays, and poems on the themes of pleasure and exploration. Roast beets with balsamic oil and pepper. Dim sum in a noisy bar. Raw avocado on a black plate. Gruyère stuck with a toothpick, dipped in local honey. Tropical slurries drizzled with liquor. Foods and experiences Lettie read about to taste, her tongue fattening in her mouth.

Nosey rested her chin on Lettie's thigh and purred. She looked less clever than the day before. Reading on, Lettie considered the onions and potatoes in the pantry, the soft celery and carrots. Cabbage. Sometimes her father brought cut beef. Most Fridays, a chicken.

When the light had traveled from the floor to the wall, middle-right to far-right, Lettie shooed Nosey to the rug and moved for her knife and pot. As she salted the water to bring on a boil, the cat rolled onto her back, legs stick-straight and splayed, while she licked her chest. Then the cat leaned her head back against the rug, almond eyes crossed briefly, before she turned onto her stomach and seized. The cat's head unhinged on its shoulders, lolling. The tongue hung out like a tiny pink flag. Lettie was so frightened by the accordion hiss that she couldn't move. She stood with her knife in her hand and waited for the cat to recover its wits, indicated by a licking of paws and the tedious nipping of lice.

FROM time to time, Frank brought ill-fitting clothes home in supermarket bags. He deposited them in a basket beneath his chair. As the soup simmered, Lettie stepped out of her pants and into a pair of purple corduroys, slack in the knees, too long. She folded up the hems and bent to her kit for matching thread. By the blazing stove, she sewed in her underpants. The bottoms of the corduroys were tattered by the rub of some person's heels. Lettie tried to visualize this person, this girl, who wore her pants too long, whose boots ground down on the fibers, but she couldn't see her, not for anything.

After dark, the temperature dropped and frost designs decorated the windows. She'd long ago abandoned her sewing and dressed again. She watched through the window as Frank's truck bounced home. Another day nearly done.

Frank wanted a moment or two alone before dinner. He hung his coat and hat on the wall and withdrew to his room where he listened to Stravinsky on cassette or tuned his radio. Lettie uncluttered the floor of her sewing and reading, softly putting things right before he emerged, a turtle from his crust. Nosey dozed on the chair.

The soup had boiled so long that most of the liquid turned to vapor. For volume, Lettie added water as her father climbed the stairs.

"No one cooks like you," he said, yanking his chair in under him.

Lettie had no way of knowing whether anyone cooked like her, or if she cooked like anyone else.

"Something unusual happened today," she said. "Nosey lost all control. She seized."

"How horrible," Frank said. He left his spoon balanced on his bowl and went to the cat. She lifted her sleeping head and opened her eyes. "You say she seized?"

"Something. It didn't seem right to me."

"Wait and watch. That's the advice for something like this.

She looks fine to me. But watch her." He rubbed the cat beneath her chin and behind her ears. She appeared to love him in the same way Lettie did, for his courtesies. Yet those same courtesies—that irking politeness—also led to Lettie's frustration. Lettie was made uncomfortable by the rush and build-up of her emotions, because the decorum of their life required her to keep anything intense in check.

"Couldn't you take her to work with you? Maybe someone can look at her."

"It's not like that," he said.

"You see people. Maybe someone knows something that can help her."

"Nobody knows anything," he said, ending the conversation.

After dinner Frank sat in his chair, staring at the fire. Lettie cleared the bowls and ran the faucet. The water was shock cold over her fingers, stiffening her flesh and the blood inside. She placed the clean pot, bowls, and spoons on the shelf above the sink and set the teakettle to bubble on the fire.

On with the routine.

"Do you have any requests?" she asked her father.

"'An Otherworldly Delight.' 1997. *The Times*. Also 'A Glimpse of Magnificence and Genius.' 1995, I believe. *The New Yorker*. And, well, surprise me. You pick one."

Lettie gathered the binder and a handful of journals from the shelf. A chill crept along the floorboards from Frank's room, ghosting across the exposed skin of her back. She moved closer to the stove and shuffled the papers. A final clump of potato dissolved on her tongue. Next, a nugget of sugary carrot. The cabbage slaw was like veins in her teeth.

Frank crossed his legs and leaned forward on his topmost knee. Like always, Lettie began to read.

HER name: Carolyn Brody Taylor. Born in 1974 and raised in Waltham Forest by a banker and a legal secretary. After completing secondary school, she trained classically, the Cecchetti method, in London for a number of years before moving overseas. Her calling as a dancer was brief. All counted, there were seven productions, each with the New York City Ballet. She was known for her strength, her fantastic ability to appear suspended, a hovering body in the illusion of flight.

She suffered a career-ending spinal injury in 1998.

When Lettie was younger, her father allowed her to twirl and twirl until the floor gave way. "Imagine what your mum felt like after the injury," he said. Frank told her that together they'd wandered the Eastern coastline like nomads for months and years, eventually finding Danceland. In Lettie's reoccurring dream she came upon an ethereal blizzard of dancers on the beach. Red tutus against white sand. Though easily she could visualize the taffeta and tulle, her mother's face and features were always nondescript; Carolyn was a brunette blur of shifting appearance.

Sadly, Lettie was naturally thick. Even in her dreams a fist of fat could be pulled from her inner thigh. Books dictate that though some things can be denied, we are made from parts of our parents, and Lettie naturally wanted to know what of her was whose. When she was a girl, Frank told these stories: whirling with operas, the dank cloud of cigarettes smoked under a shared umbrella, gilded doves amid dimmed lights, sunrises, taxicabs, and her mum's pink ballet flats rolled into a soft leathery ball. But as she grew older, if she asked, her father reduced his gaze and said, "It's not a worthy pursuit, this line of questions. It's impossible to have all knowledge." Only gently, at teatime, or if she were very ill, could she ask a simple question. Eventually Lettie realized she knew all she was to know about her mother, and about Danceland.

WHEN it was cold they retired early. Frank touched her forehead with his lips, the same spot every night; you would think the skin would dull. He smelled like nothing but himself: warm flannel, the outdoors come inside, ballpoint pen, two-days-unwashed hair.

Every night he said, "See you in the ante meridiem." He meant morning.

"Do you think she'll be okay?" Lettie asked. The cat stopped briefly on the stairs to peek out the window for fox or raccoon. Cats do not stargaze.

Frank said, "I think we'll see her in the ante meridiem too," and passed Lettie her oil lamp. He turned with his to descend the stairs, dismissing her with his free hand.

Lettie's lamp lit the path to her room, the thick and blackened chimney casting shadows. Cool air greeted her behind the closed door. Low eaves on each side, there was area enough in her room for a bed and trunk, a small bookcase, and the commode chair. She set the lamp on the windowsill, so she could see herself reflected. She would have liked to see in her reflection the color of her eyes or the definition of her cheekbones, but each night she was nothing more than a glowing mass in the dark.

She pulled the elastic bands from her hair and loosened her long braids into a crimped heap which she combed as in ritual. First working the kinks at the bottom, then reaching to the top and pulling the comb over the whole mess. Hundreds of strokes. She liked the way her scalp prickled. Nosey sat on her lap and Lettie teased the cat with her own tail of hair before wrapping it into place.

Heat rose to her room through the grate in the floor. She opened the metal slot and warmed her feet as she dressed for sleep, leaving her day clothes on top of her trunk. Sliding on thermals and wool socks. Settling into the flannel bedding, pink quilt, crochet frill. She liked to think that she slept in her mother's marriage bed.

The cat leaped up and lengthened against her, nuzzling Lettie's chest. Her green eyes slits against the lamplight, an ancient profile that reminded Lettie of a book on Cleopatra's court. Lettie stroked the cat until it purred, occasionally stretching arms and legs taut then loose. She kissed the cat's ears and let her hand hover over its hip.

In the moment, Lettie was afraid Nosey was arranging to die. In the moment, everything accelerated: her heart, her thoughts. Images sped toward her, past her: the peeling porch door, an airplane overhead, a fever rag, red clay chipping off Frank's boots in the entry, a woman's face, another woman's face, another woman's face. She settled on the woodpile in summer, where ants traveled in formation. Where did they go? Could she—*would she*—follow?

Down the stairs and down the stairs again, Frank slept in his stone box which glistened with frozen rivulets of the groundwater that had seeped inside. Heat didn't descend to his room, so with his blanket pulled to his chin, Lettie's father breathed in the cold copper scent and breathed out something else. He slept in total quiet, everything unyielding. But he dreamed; Lettie was sure of it.

NOSEY was not well, same with her, and then the airplane ripped into view. The concurrence of these factors seemed meant to be, necessary, somehow fatal.

She came to the place where the vapor trail was obscured by the dark canopy above and pushed on through the woods, passing the soft, mossy streams, encountering rabbits and squirrels alert and afraid, mid-motion. Like a girl in a fable, she ate bread and cheese from a napkin in her pocket, sucking the pulp from the wild blueberries that dotted the low vegetation. Rickety clapboard houses. Stone foundations teeming with beetles and spiders. A wide muddy road. She walked throughout the day until dark, when she climbed a tree, and settled into a cradle of branches. Unable to sleep, she watched an owl in the moonlight, hearing trees creak in the wind, the sound evoking a nightmare image of so many bodies hanging from nooses. All night she heard the fevered ghosts wailing in the trees and by morning, though she was weary, she felt mission-driven.

The woods thinned into a grove of lofty pines, the ground smothered under a rug of brown needles. Up above, the moon showed nearly full, the sun ready to set in the west. A stone wall, thousands of head-sized rocks, thrust through the grove and pointed to an incline.

She followed the wall, using roots to steady herself and resorting to all fours when it became too steep. Partway up, heart thumping, she stopped to rest, her lungs hot and tight. Down below, she heard timber crack.

Three boys, no older than her, filled the grove with activity, one hopping on a thick branch and pulling up to make the splitting sound, another putting a bush knife to a tree trunk, the last pissing, a slight penis in his cupped hand.

It hadn't occurred to her that she'd find boys her own age. Older men with orange vests, sure. More like it: a woman with her children.

The boys crowded together. Three bodies, a pinwheel.

She grasped a branch, steadying herself before descending. But her shoe slipped on a loose stone. She cried out as she tumbled to a stop, her head hitting the stone wall.

As the boys clambered toward her, her shame took wet shape in tears and blood. Dark earth clung to the fibers of Frank's sweater.

The boy with the knife came close. "Head down," he ordered, and parted her hair. "Does it hurt?"

She told him it hurt, but that she was sure she'd be fine. She asked him where they were.

"You don't know where you are?" he said. She looked at the shoes of the other boys. Cleaner, newer than any she'd ever worn. "You're just up the path from the Palmers' farm. Where do you live?"

How to answer? She'd already decided that the crooked, shingled cottage in the woods wasn't home—not anymore at least.

"I'm lost," she said, repeating the words she'd practiced. "I think I need help."

"You say you're lost?"

The boy who'd pissed was nervously kicking up large rocks, one after another.

"I'll call," said the other, who'd split the branch.

The throbbing pain in her head distorted her vision. One moment the pines were there in excruciatingly realistic detail and the next the pines were vague pillars collapsing into oblivion. She closed her eyes and slipped into Danceland. Her mother's soft, clean, and strong hands slicing cheese on a patchwork quilt in the meadow; then slippery spit at the corner of the cat's mouth; finally her father dangling from a tree, a silhouette against the burning cottage. Everything ablaze and disintegrating.

FRANK

YEAR AFTER YEAR, Frank's mother pointed to the nest, a dark gathering in a tree at the park. He remembered racing toward the tree to check for it in all weather. Summer, the tangle rested on the lush pillow of vegetation. Winter, it was suspended, twigs clinging to one another. But the wind did not shake it. Snow and ice did not weigh it down. It persisted. Frank would squint against the sun seeing not a true nest, not woven by a bird's instinct, but a witch's broom, a dense mass of shoots caused by disease or insects, even possibly by someone pruning incorrectly. Certainly, some birds and animals might perch to rest, a few to settle, but it was not to be confused with a true nest, no matter what his mother called it.

Today, he knew that the technical term was "dieback." After you entered the west gate to the nature reserve, the long driveway leading to the parking area was lined with mature American ash, each cankerous, leaves spotted, witch's brooms emerging one or three to a tree.

Below, Frank's assistant Eric stood with arms akimbo, surveying the meadow. Frank adjusted the lift and his helmet as he pulled himself closer to a mass of fresh shoots.

The trustees and management insisted on trimming without damaging the structure of the trees, the pleasantly canopied passage to the park. Frank predicted that the ash would be dead in a decade or less. New growth would take that long at least. Still, he cut only the minor branches, close to the collar, and applied fungicide to the wounds, both those he made and those the tree had already suffered.

Eric picked up his rake and waved the curious driver on. "Park's open. No fee today," he said. To Frank, as the driver's window rolled back up, he said, "Don't these people work?"

"Tourists," Frank said. On a good day, Frank used no more than seventy-five words, which included those for conversation with Lettie, something she required. But the seventy-five did not include lies. Lies were free. On a bad day, Frank said too much and nervousness made it difficult to sleep.

"I wish I didn't have to work," Eric said. He'd already told Frank that he was saving his summer earnings to buy his neighbor's Jeep, so that he could transfer to the technical school in the fall, which required a car. It was still May.

Eric prepared to hoist the shears up the tree.

Frank worked thoughtfully, checking every set of branches for its leader and trimming the others back, the chosen one and the ones Frank chose to pass on. When he was finished he loosened the lift and slowly descended.

Eric had already gathered the debris on a tarp and hauled it all to the bed of the truck. There, he'd started the engine and now waited.

Frank slid the harnesses from the carabiners and stepped out, then coiled his ropes and rigging into a box in the truck.

Inside the truck, Eric listened to a college station out of Boston. Frank didn't mind the radio, but was embarrassed by the positivity of the kids' voices, the lilt of fantastic opportunity. He remembered peering into that particular station window, which faced Boston Common, as the students took turns playing disc jockey, lucky to have the airwaves from Boston to the Berkshires. Frank didn't turn the radio off; he turned it down. Had Eric put on news radio, Frank would have shut it off. But Eric hadn't, and wouldn't.

"Don't you have anyone in your life turning you on to new music?" Eric said.

The sun warmed Frank's forearms and hands on the wheel. It was near enough to noon that he suggested they break for lunch. "I'll drop you at the booth," he said. Eric clearly had a thing with one of the staff. Frank had seen them crouched in the bushes, smoking. Eric passing the joint to her long, freckled hand. She reminded Frank of someone. He suspected that her parents must be livid.

Even when it rained, for lunch Frank went to the municipal airport, his truck parked beneath the flag. He nodded at the greeter, a thick-cheeked woman with a perpetual run in her nylons. The donut machine, backlit with a scratched neon tube, was stocked on Tuesdays, Thursdays, and Saturdays. Glazed, chocolate glazed, so-called strawberry "jimmies," and jelly stuffed. He preferred old-fashioned, the subtle scent of fried dough, cinnamon and butter, the entire sugary sponge dipped in machine-made coffee.

A row of wicker rocking chairs and side tables were arranged by the window. Frank sat and watched the action of a prop plane getting ready to take-off. The airport facilities provided for recreation and instruction, as well as for the occasional corporate or military landing. For the most part, it was a place for enthusiasts. Frank watched a woman and man ready for flight. Jackets zipped and gloves pulled on. Their plane looked like a toy. A white thunderbolt painted over a red metal body. The blades of the propeller decorated too. Frank had never seen a pilot who didn't look slightly cocky. He had no desire to fly. What he was looking for, he did not know. Just, he appreciated the cannon-ball explosion of first ignition and the scream of take-off.

HERE was another puzzle: rhododendrons in the forest were left to sprawl over any outcropping they rooted toward; yet, rhododendrons planted just so between the stone foundation of the nature center and gracious brick patio are pruned annually, stunted back to a third of their size, looking like arms-length balls bouncing on bark mulch. True, plants don't know, but the falseness nagged Frank.

Frank saw the girl kiss Eric and pop his collar. "It's ridiculous," his assistant said. "The way she thinks I'm a certain sort of person."

"What sort of person does she think you are?"

"Some kind of athlete, I guess."

Frank and Eric carried their equipment from the truck—shears and a tarp—and began to work in the afternoon sun.

Frank figured Eric was afraid of his echo. He kept talking so he would never hear what he'd just said. School, his parents, the girl. His life didn't exist if he didn't talk about it. Frank's life, on the other hand, would cease to exist if he ever spoke of it. His daughter, protected, untouched. Constantly, he considered whether she was ready. Ready to know. Ready to go. He considered whether he was ready, and he never was. She had the voracious desire to believe. She didn't even ask.

In his endless monologue, Eric did ask questions: *Australian? British, then? Your folks, where are they living? So sorry, when did they pass? Whereabouts is your house? What road,*

I mean. Like a greedy bird, Eric pecked. But Frank had become resourceful, adept at squatting, twisting, climbing. He cut Eric off just as he sawed down the dead or dangerous branches of very old trees.

Though initially he attracted attention, no doubt due to his accent, he knew how to put people off. Actually, most people lost interest in him quickly when he didn't take much of an interest in them. He drifted, hanging close to the doors.

Unlike the Bostonians he'd known, he found that except for the youth, the people living in the western area of the state were composed, even dispassionate. Not long ago, Frank drove past a devastating house fire on his way to the nature reserve. On the television news, turned on in the break room, a man in his middle age, clothed in a relaxed flannel jacket, was being interviewed. Without a flap of emotion he said his dog saved him. Behind him, in the view, you could see the blackened beams of the construction still smoking. Everything soot. The man held the dog and said, "Sure is a good dog."

ERIC was a zealous trimmer, Frank's supervisor had warned. The supervisor said Eric's mother must have praised him for eating his whole supper or tidying his trinkets and that was why. But, oh, the sparse hedges. Frank had been instructed to teach Eric the difference between neatness and beauty. He cast a shadow over Eric's shears, enfolding his assistant momentarily to indicate the contrast between this and next summer's buds, the tight hearts falling. When Eric began to make good cuts with regularity, Frank moved on to the next bush, the gravel nicking beneath his boots.

Eric was his first assistant. Prior, he'd been the assistant. But Black died suddenly of an alcoholic's seizure when he tried to stop drinking on his own. Now, Frank worked every day with Eric to recreate the companionable silence he and Black had shared. He remembered fondly Black wiping woodchips from his knees, saying, "Keep it clean, keep it clean." At the end of the day, Black would drag a case of beer between his knees.

Six years of silence. Black had it: the attitude, the New England nonchalance. It was essential.

Eric was talking about the international supermarket where the deli sold falafel and sushi side by side. "It's like being from someplace else is fashionable," he said. "I don't know, maybe it is."

"Maybe it is," Frank said.

"Well, you would know. Is this place, like, Nowheresville or what?"

"It's nice here. Very pleasant."

"Everyone who lives here wants out, obviously."

Frank had come to learn that when you live in a place long enough you begin to pick up the rhythm of its life; the culture begins to transform you, even if your accent sticks. People travel—cross-country, cross-continent. If most men in the world are uprooted for war, what is life like for them in Afghanistan? In Iraq? The British still have bases outside Moscow and in Vietnam too. Humanitarian work. In the seventies, the Space Age, the conflict over nuclear supremacy, made it possible to break out of Earth's atmosphere, albeit for a short time. How had weightlessness changed the earliest explorers? Not just of our solar system, but also of our rivers and oceans?

Here was Frank though. Here in the Berkshires, in a crooked shack, where people let the pain pass right over them and go elsewhere. Just go. They shop thrift. They eat their vegetables fresh and dirty. They complain more about the nail sticking out of the front steps than they do about Communism and terrorism, oil and nukes. Frank's wars were all internal now.

THE breeze, strong from the south, shook the forsythia hedge. Frank agitated the branches too. *Wake up, all of you.* The trustees preferred to hire only specialists. Frank's job was thus limited. Still, he felt the burden of the property. A badly rotted pergola. A marble statue, one of the last true sculptures, balanced on a crumbling concrete stand. Why, he wondered, had the original owner chosen so much concrete, not just for the edges and walls, but also for the lovely benches and figurine? It wasn't art if it was made from a mold. Frank's mind worked that way: moving from the wrong things he could fix to the wrong things no one could. He couldn't stop his thoughts from racing in that direction.

Eric brought in the corners of the tarp and hauled it to the mulch pile.

The night stretched ahead. They punched their cards in the clock. Give or take a few minutes, the guttural tick was the same. Frank nodded at the volunteer behind the information desk, a befuddled aide always crumbling a cookie on a napkin.

"Night Frankie," she said.

"Night Bernie," he said, two words to make a pathetic woman smile. *Night* and her name.

In the parking lot Frank watched as Eric helped his girlfriend fold the A-frame welcome sign and slide shut the windows of the booth for the evening. "Don't forget to lock it," she directed him as she carried her cashbox inside. He remembered the feeling of being told what to do.

Frank drove around the circle and down through the ash

trees, slowly to admire his work. Then the long way home. Down Rice Hill, squeezing the curve. Past the elementary school and playground, where some children chased. Over the bridge, seeing the moss turning the town's earliest gravestones green. To his right, the burned home of the man and dog.

The question that had been forming in his mind all day finally clarified: can a person who has already disappeared *actually* disappear?

The paved road ended. A gate was left open. On either side: stumps, logs, granite boulders. Clay and dirt made up the path that Frank continued along. The truck vibrated as Frank maneuvered it over the heaves and rocks, the ruts, and deeper into the forest. He'd found this place completely by chance. Lettie was first to point at the blazing yellow rooftop covered in pine needles, to toddle toward it.

It was July and they'd been based at a lonely campground, one hundred and fifty miles outside Boston, since May. He'd stacked their belongings in a prepaid cedar-smelling unit at a Roxbury storage facility. He'd ordered a post-office box. He'd said to his mother, gently, gently, "Please, just let me go," and she'd listened. They paid cash by the week to stay in a rented trailer with an attached aluminum screen porch. Lettie slept in a bunk with a plastic rail.

Living there with a young child was like living anywhere with a young child. They ate off the same plate. They nattered at each other. They made each other laugh by making extraordinary noises. In the city when Lettie bellyached, Frank would strap her into a carrier and walk. Being in the woods was no different. Hiking ten miles here, nine miles there, through the area's deserted region.

Goodbye.

By the looks of the front walk, the wobbling stones were

meant to cohere, but hundreds of storms had pushed up mud, and that mud had gathered strength and pushed the round rocks apart. Frank had knocked. He'd beckoned any ghosts to greet him. But not even a spirit occupied the house. All it had was the mood. Comforting creaks. The smooth and cool enamel of the wood cookstove. Its quiet assurance that here, in these horsehair walls, they'd be just fine.

That night, with Lettie fed and asleep in her sack, Frank thought about the house, imagining a private future. A life apart. Overhead, an airplane passed, the pilot letting loose on the engine before landing.

ESPECIALLY in the early years, before Lettie could speak, Frank spent long hours in reverie. She played with marbles in the sun or flowers in the garden while he imagined a *life apart*, an alternate future. He and Carolyn. They were like insects reconnecting in midair, over and over again. Magnetism is a natural law. The way he saw her, everything about her had matured, strengthened. Her muscular back arching. In the dreams, Lettie tied ballet flats too. Both of them sitting with their chins in soft palms. Anyone would confuse Lettie for Carolyn's daughter. They shared zest. You could sense that their passions were refined. From the clarity of their earth-brown eyes, you could see they shared the highest ideals: beauty, truth, freedom.

He sat beside her on a log bench overlooking the falls, the entire forest on fire with the season. "What do you think, Dad?" Lettie would ask.

But then came the hallucinations, which of course he never spoke about. Delusions. His wild-headed mother, tapping her foot at the bottom of the basement steps, her hand out, "Help me." Or a busy heap under Lettie's covers, she and Eric wrestling on a bed of tree trimmings, a wrench on the side table, keys to a Jeep. And then, an accusing banshee, her mouth of rotten teeth, thumbprint bruises on her neck and arms, her stagger a clear indication of so many years still drunk. She wanted just one kiss. He imagined her giving up on a rusty cot, her mouth open to take in the salty air, let out foul spirits, a pair of gentle but worn slippers side by side beneath her.

Every year the woods crept closer. If Frank and Lettie ever left, he knew the roots would eventually search through the foundation, and move in. During winter, the snow packed down the field and stretched its not-quite square boundaries. Then in spring the matted grass sprang back. Summer passed, and here he was, opening the porch door to see a field overrun with vegetation. Every summer, a new colony of stalky, gnarly weeds. Cord-like quackgrass with its tight gathering of tiny seeds. Goldenrod loose in the breeze, a yellow blur, some of them spreading seeds softer and lighter than thoughts.

In the later years, Lettie took her books to the crook of the apple tree. He'd close his eyes, resting them, and still, a gentle blue spot danced in the vision of his left pupil. The specialist in London, long ago, had called it the "warning knock." A tender misery calling for him again.

The doctor had asked, "When did these headaches begin?"

And Frank's mother had said, "Infancy."

"Are you sure?"

"Confident," Deb said.

Soon, the blue dot would dissolve into thousands of electric globes. Soon, his pulse, the blood in his temples, would begin to rush, and as it rushed, it would expand, it would flash into his neck and shoulders, the joints in his jaw slackening, saliva pooling under and around his tongue. And on the plaid wool sofa of his childhood, he'd lie on his left side, resting his left temple on the cushion. Deb would mix orange juice with something fizzy, bring two sleeping pills. Frank chewed them, the vile chalk sticking in the crevices of his molars. He'd lean into the bin to vomit. His mother would hurry to wash it, her hands pushed into rubber gloves that reached her sleeves. She'd say, "Sleep. Sleep. Frankie, just please fall asleep," as if she could not stand the pain.

And he would. He'd rest against the woolen cushion, close his eyes, feeling his very consciousness rocking from left to right, up to the heights and down into the depths. He was a boy, a body, adrift at sea, knocking in the surf.

HE wrote and received letters at the post-office box. Carolyn left New York to recover in Los Angeles, where her most recent letter said she still lived. Frank wanted to call her Carrie or, more fondly, Care. But he didn't. He called her Carolyn. Carolyn Taylor not Carolyn Brody, out of respect. He knew the jacarandas were blooming and wondered whether her husband—Trent was his name—pushed her wheelchair, if she could enjoy the purple flush outside the Philharmonic. He didn't include a postscript. It had nothing to do with saying too much. The words in his letters to Carolyn were free; they didn't count at end of day. It was just that the frivolousness was over between them, the postscript.

What began as an impulsive missive, written and sent in lonely haste, became an easy obsession, light and regular communication, his only with his other life. In the early years, Frank was loose about the letters, leaving them on the counter and bureau. In this way, Carolyn talked with him in every room. Lettie was too young to reach or know. At that time, Frank rarely left home either. He and Lettie crawled after centipedes chasing the floorboards, and outside, after the butterflies in the buddleia. When she was one year old, she learned to eat what was sown in the field, what grew on the trees and bushes. When she was two, she learned to count with daisy petals and change from his pockets. Nickels were her favorite. When she was three, she developed an imaginary friend named Mum. Mum's hair was three times longer than the length of her legs and she wore it in a French twist. That was when Frank collected Carolyn's letters in a box that he slid beneath the basement eaves. By the time she was four, Frank had introduced her to the idea of Carolyn, and she began to learn to read from newspaper clippings about the proud dancer who'd fallen down.

Frank sat with his daughter on the rug by the stove. He kept the door open sometimes. He liked the smoke in his throat.

"Read the story again," Lettie would say.

"This one about The Firebird?"

"The Firebird." Here, his daughter lived across the ocean and still she sounded British. In isolation Frank supposed anything could be learned.

He'd read the articles so often that they were memorized. The words and images tumbled from his mouth. He'd never seen Carolyn dance, but he could imagine.

He wrote letters to her, shaped his emotions into subtleties. He transcribed the day-to-day. She was impossible to lie to, so he never tried. He told her how he lived with her, how Lettie did too, in the everyday.

And, as if she didn't realize what that meant, Frank noted that she never told anyone. As if she had no concerns about a young girl living in a rickety shack, he trusted Carolyn to never send anyone to look, to prevent what was happening from happening. Frank appreciated that she left it like it was, almost as if she preferred it this way.

As a child Lettie had loved everything about Carolyn. She loved in the same way a girl could love a puppet or a storybook heroine. A vast and colorful dreamscape patterned Lettie's childhood. Carolyn was the focus of her imagination. And like most children she perseverated on small details: what color ribbon Carolyn tied in her hair, which composers she preferred. She delighted in minute similarities she could strike between herself and Carolyn. Knowing this, Frank made some up. He embellished. He dreamed a sweet and satisfying dream in which Carolyn was his wife, his daughter's mother, and he shared the dream with Lettie.

Based on her experiences, he assumed his daughter figured that death occurred in one of two ways. The first was what she called "pause." She'd found examples among insects in particular, but also in birds and other wildlife residing in the woods. When she turned eight, she asked him about "pause," and he told her he could think of no good explanation for it. "Pause" was beyond their comprehension. The second cause of death was a snapped spine, the protrusion of backbone. This, she intimated from what she knew about Carolyn. She'd existed. She'd been a mother. A dancer. She'd snapped her spine. She didn't exist anymore. Lettie was cautious in her work and play. She was sturdy and slow in her movement. Then, two days before Lettie disappeared, the cat seized again. Frank had begun to worry that now he would need to explain other causes of death. Infestation. Disease. Decay.

He parked outside the sheriff's department to report his daughter's disappearance. They would want to know what she looked like. Somehow he could not picture her in whole, like she'd become a person he hadn't seen in a very long time. He remembered her in slices. A figure sometimes thick, always resolute. Dirt under her thin and peeling fingernails. The pair of pink leather ballet slippers he gave her when she turned six. She hung them on a peg in the hall, even after they had worn thin. She gathered onion skin and tossed it in the yard. Her eyes, at first violet, eventually turned smooth brown. The soft wisdom in her gaze. Her pant legs rolled up to reveal bruised calves. The day she defied him and stayed outside during a rainstorm, squatting in a muddy puddle, smiling up into the shower. Dusty knees with light blonde hair you might only notice in bright light. A bee sting on the knuckle of her big toe that swelled up badly. The way she held her hands over her chest, once she grew breasts. Freckles on her forehead and nose beginning as early as April every year. The cautious determination she showed when learning to walk, her solid movement on round and fat bare feet. She might be five feet. She might be one hundred pounds. She had recently turned twelve years old.

Frank opened the glass door and waited in the dimly lit lobby for the sheriff's receptionist to ask him what she could do to help.

Part Two

DANCING

FRANK

HE HADN'T ALWAYS been a remote man. Frank grew into his life. He had his family. When he was a young child, his father worked upstairs in the library, computing at a wide, round table, and his mother hurried Frank down the stone steps to the village. At the depot, she gave him warm pennies with which to buy a bag of salted black licorice. He'd pay and meet his mother at the fountain, where she stood with her hand shielding her eyes from the sun, surveying the square. They walked on. In warm weather the shopkeepers brought sale racks to the street and sat nearby on worn wooden chairs. Deb loved new stock, but more, she loved seasonal sales. Frank would press his fingers into the window boxes, testing the sponginess of the soil, a cord of licorice melting between his molars. Other boys played jacks on the corner, sped by on their bicycles, and climbed the public works sculptures. But Frank waited. He waited for his mother, just to hear the way she'd thank the salesgirl, the genuinely warm *au revoir.* And by morning's end, Deb would have gratefully assembled a number of waxed paper bags on her forearms. As they made their way out of the square, she'd offer money to the vagrants, and swing her bags.

Bags carrying blouses and accessories, dining linens, guest room soaps. They thanked her. And she wished them well. When she and Frank got home, she'd quickly slide her purchases into the darkness of the cupboard and noisily ask Frank about supper. She'd say, "Your father will be starving."

He had his school, where when he'd reached a certain level of maturity, he was recruited to tutor a young woman who never wanted to work. One afternoon she said she'd misplaced her textbook, so Frank reviewed her work at the dining room table while she went to her bedroom to look. She'd written a paper for Victorian Britain on the Potato Famine in Ireland. She wrote: "The actions—and inactions—of the British government worsened the natural disaster, killing a million people over the course of four years." He checked his book, and though she hadn't copied it word for word, clearly she'd lifted the statement. He could hear her in the other room, talking on the phone; he pictured her in there, wrapping the cord around her wrists and hands till she cut off circulation. He waited.

He waited by opening the envelope he'd ordered from Amnesty International. Out slid a notecard. It said: *Celebrate 20 Years*. And it pictured twenty candles, all blown out. Beneath the picture, it said: *End Political Killings*. The first was the staple-bound pamphlet, "Campaign Against Torture," which included a twelve-point plan. The second was the toolkit for educators, "Teaching and Learning about Human Rights."

He flipped through the charts while his classmate chattered in her bedroom. She had a way of whispering when she said something negative about someone else. Whenever she phoned, to reschedule a session or ask a question about the work, she'd lower her voice to speak about her mother. She'd murmur, "My mother—*she thinks she knows everything*—has decided you should come read this." Or, "The queen—*you know, my mother*—doesn't realize they already passed the Factory Act and told me to phone." When she was saying things this way to Frank, he did feel closer to her, but as he overheard her now, lowering her voice to talk, he remembered the divide between them. By six o'clock, he realized she wasn't coming out, and he quickly rephrased her main point and some of the supporting information, then marked her mistakes before leaving. Later that night she phoned and spoke softly, "Mr. Greggs can be such an arse about copying."

Frank had his options. Near the end of secondary school, in the English office, Miss Harriman rolled her chair away from her desk and crossed her legs. She wore a white blouse with a long, tan corduroy skirt. Frank thought her ankles were her best feature, the round and slim meeting of foot and firm leg. The way they bobbed beneath her desk as she led class. But he also respected her knowledge, and generosity. The impulses were in opposition and he was never at ease in her presence.

Frank sat in the chair beside her desk. It belonged in the library, at one of the oblong tables.

"What's next for you? What's after this?" she asked. "I won't tolerate this Peace Corps nonsense."

Frank's classmates—most of them—were enrolling at the local university. He'd applied to join the Peace Corps or to attend a program in the States, in Boston. He could do either.

His teacher said, "You're not a flake, are you?"

Frank flinched. He said, "I'm not a flake."

"You're not a slouch."

"No."

"Your parents and I don't want postcards from Tanzania."

Really, Frank had always felt he had no options, none at all. All were artificial, false, imagined. And so he wouldn't stand up; he'd yield. Frank had always been a person who yielded. To the presence of a stronger attitude, of a desire more intense than his own. And this is how he came to the determination that no matter what options presented themselves, none were true, because a wiser decision had already been made by someone other than himself. And so, as that summer spread out before him, and Carolyn Brody Taylor danced in and out of his life, he was disappointed, yes, but also resigned, resigned to watching his life play out.

FOUR years later, after a private commencement ceremony, Frank's parents waited below the cross signal, a white hand blinking on the other side of the street. His parents were dressed conservatively except for his mother's shoes—unreasonable heels she tested on the flow and rise, the crack and crumble of century-old brick walkways.

The ten Peace Fellows—as the anonymous donor who'd funded the program referred to them—received their diplomas during a simple ceremony in the dean's personal library, on the ground level of a brownstone on Beacon Hill, near the State House.

His closest friend had already been hired for an assignment in Asia, and had flown out the week earlier, pledging to write. Frank wasn't close with the others, could not relate to their sheer optimism and he thought meaningless volunteerism, the falseness of their charity. Despite his feelings for them, Frank had earned the respect of his peers and faculty for his cool demeanor and eloquence. A problem presented and the calmest argument took shape—letter by letter, every potentiality—behind his eyes and passing through his lips like a smooth breeze. Frank was not the kind of person who would say the wrong thing, when later the right thing would come to mind.

He met his parents across the street and led them down the hill to Charles Street, where he'd reserved a dinner table. His mother complained about her ankles, but once they reached the shop fronts, she quieted. The shining apples in the cart outside the co-op. The scent of starch in the steam from the cleaner. Shining silver timepieces and tureens displayed on red velvet. Letterpressed stationary. His mother was a specialist in fine things. In buying fine things.

He'd picked the restaurant on that basis. It wasn't a place he'd been to before, but he'd passed by, late nights walking with cigarettes, noticing the formal settings, the refined glow of candlelight, the precision and maturity of the waiters.

As they settled into their seats and opened their menus, Frank checked his parents. His father had new lines, not from laughing. His mother's hair was professionally blown up into a hollow bun.

They chattered civilly about the hotel in Copley Square and about the changes on Boylston Street since their last visit. The waiter came and went. A warm boule was served with carved butter roses.

His father coughed into his sleeve and said, "I suppose you'll come home."

Frank said, "I'd like to work in the States a few years and see then."

"Marshall Smith says he has an opening," his mother said. "Merchant banking."

Frank considered his words, finally saying, "I'm not trained for that."

"That's not an issue."

In the years he'd lived away from home he'd labeled himself: misfit, bore, failure. He'd labeled his father: distracted, money-hungry, absent. He'd labeled his mother: co-dependent, silly, thriftless.

"Thomas and Andrew are home. Both working at Smith Brothers," she said.

Frank knew that his mother meant to say *she* was home. If *she* was home, wasn't that where *he* owed it to her to be? Frank figured home meant something else, something more complex. He'd left his parents' home even before he actually departed, before he stepped on the plane. He'd been gone from Debra's home since he'd met Carolyn the summer before school. At the pub where he was a busboy, she'd been wiping her spill on the counter with her scarf when he slid a stack of serviettes her way. "Don't mess your lovely scarf." Later, after his shift ended and her friends left, he sat across from her in a booth. She opened and closed a purple cocktail umbrella the same way she opened and closed her velvet eyes. Blinking slowly. She had a new hole in her heart. A man had promised he'd take her south and then . . . Next thing Frank knew, he'd pulled the car around to the front of the pub, snatched the traveler's checks from his father's safe, and before remembering to leave a note, he'd already driven Carolyn two hours to Sussex Downland, finding a sheep farm dug into a rolling seaside valley. Shortly after daybreak, they checked into a guesthouse where they swayed in and out of days softly in a hammock. She picked wild irises and knit socks with farm-spun wool. They ate cheese and fresh honey. He admired her red hair as the sun set. But Frank was impatient.

One evening, he asked her to go with him to the States. But she had her dance scholarship in London, another future, one that didn't involve Frank, even if he gave her everything every other man had not. She said, "I won't forget you." And three weeks later Frank flew to the States, independent and foul.

He knew it would be painful for his mother to hear, that he'd hurt her by saying it, so *gently, gently*, he said, "I think I'll stay."

"'To each their own' is what I always say, isn't it?" And she sucked her spoon.

They finished their meals in silence. Frank spread his potatoes and gravy thin. He sliced his beef this way and that. He thought of the cow.

His father said a few ominous words about his U.S. banking affairs as he passed his credit card to the waiter.

FRANK'S supervisor at the telephone outreach center, Ladette, was three months younger than him. He'd been hired two weeks before, and after their shift they mixed gimlets in his apartment, skipped dinner, and discussed their birth dates in bed. She considered herself mature for her age. For whatever reason, Ladette was not a kisser and had preferred sex the *other* way. He'd looked over the back of her head. Her scalp showed through the thin, gloomy hair, but Ladette's muscularity and stamina had startled Frank.

"Not that I take that job seriously, but could you please not mention this?" Ladette later said.

"Of course. I wouldn't."

"No?" She was Midwestern, some small factory town she may have mentioned at his interview. She pulled without apology at her necklace, bringing the gold charm to her chest and the clasp back to her neck. "Not worth mentioning?"

"I don't mean it like that."

"Sure. Whatever you say, Frank."

LADETTE required her people to arrive fifteen minutes before the shift's start. She never said whether this was agency policy or her own. She issued warnings, written on yellow-lined note cards. Frank spent mornings in bed and haunted the Coop's magazine offerings after lunch, attending the occasional poetry collection signing. By evening he was vacant and keen for the structure that work with Ladette provided. He was always early.

Pay was based on petitions verbally signed and, more importantly, by funds raised. He'd proven himself skilled at this, so by his third week his pay was well above the minimum. He kept a cubby by the window and sterilizing wipes in the drawer. The computer buzzed, an old tower, familiar from his youth, tan plastic the color and texture of years-old grunge. He sat in a swivel seat, which he'd adjusted weeks before. He kept a handwritten log of rejoinders above the monitor, which he referred to from time to time.

What he was selling was economic justice, he'd told his mother, who said there were plenty of telemarketing jobs in London.

If Frank was a salesperson, Ladette was an inventor, building intense belief in mission among a crack team of otherwise incredulous recent college graduates. The day shift could be flabby, but the night shift needed to be robust, convincing, in control. There were only fifteen days left in the legislative cycle, hundreds of thousands of dollars to raise, to close one clutch loophole.

Ladette worked up a chart at the whiteboard and Frank dialed in to the system. The chart showed each caller's progress, plusses and nils, adding up to a smile or a frown. He coughed. Five yesses in a row, three of which started as nos. One no, followed by one yes, followed by two nos. Ladette's chart showed a turned-down smile for Frank's progress. He needed to turn it back up. Occasionally, without warning, she patched in to listen, "for training purposes."

The night before, after their drinks and athletics, Frank had completely lost himself to Ladette's memories of her youth as a competitive gymnast. She'd been a tumbler. He imagined her hard and petite, in a glittering bodysuit, feet bare and dusty. She described a ledge built in to her childhood bedroom where she'd replaced her dolls, one by one, with trophies. He'd reached for the stem of her wobbling glass and placed it on the table. He tasted the lime on her tongue. Her hips were a gymnast's. She said she still nursed stress fractures in her shins and ankles.

She leaned over his shoulder and pulled the headpiece from his ear. She whispered, "Score a touchdown. Score one."

He turned around and smiled through the rap he was giving to the person on the other end, who'd just said hello.

"What are your thoughts on the abuse of the Freedom of Information act?"

The man, who may have been in his late teens or early twenties, who may have been high on heroin or meth, who may have been foreign-born, said, "Man, what you do is wrong."

"Excuse me?" Frank said.

"What you do is so wrong. You know what? We're going to send a chainsaw massacre."

"I'm sorry. I don't understand."

"Buzz down your doors. Buzz down your life," the man was saying. Frank's mind worked almost in reverse, zeroing in first on the rusty teeth of the chainsaw and then pulling back, pulling back, until he clearly saw the bloody implication of the speaker's horrible threat. He quickly, shakily, keyed the button to end the call. The rest of the shift was a bust. Frank thought of ways to slow down the exchanges, to concentrate on what people were actually saying when they were saying no, but he never earned a smiling face on Ladette's chart, not that night and not again.

Ladette said, "Listen, you can't let one nutbag ruin your run. It's your run, not his."

In her attempt to increase, enhance, and improve, Ladette had failed to see what had really happened, what *was* really happening to him, and to society. She'd blocked out everything beyond her gymnastics mat. And Frank saw then how tacky her middle-class, middle-American determination truly was. How the bother of social justice aged her. She pulled from a folder on her desk a double-sided list of common counters, ones that didn't work if you no longer believed.

F R A N K had been prepared for his mother to die, but not his father. His whole life, he had been priming. Debra would of course perish from a slow-spreading disease, a condition caused by a longstanding hint—too much sugar, too many cigarettes. But Debra did not die. Instead, Frank's father had unwrapped a biscuit while driving and hit the rail at a bend in the road, the impact causing the car to ride up and flip into the muddy gulch below. Frank's mother hadn't been able to locate him the rest of the day, nor that night. She said she wouldn't call the office. When busy at work, his father had a short temper. Much earlier in the marriage she'd learned to wait, not to call. He would come home when he came home. The end. In the morning someone phoned her. By afternoon, Frank was adjusting his seat as the airplane navigated a heat storm over the Atlantic, headed for London.

You spend your whole life planning for one thing and then something else happens. Because she refused to get into a car any time soon, early the next day Frank left his mother in her bed and drove his rental car to the mortuary to receive his father's ashes.

His father's parents and siblings all had proper burials in the parish yard. His father, an atheist by the age of ten, had noted clearly in his papers that he preferred cremation, and did not specify where the ashes were to be spread, just that he did not want to be buried in the ground.

The car park was full, so Frank exited and parked along the street under a willow. He weaved through the people grieving on the steps and patio, telling a man with a nametag that he had come for his father's remains. "I'll wait here," Frank said.

"You need to sign. I'm sorry, but there's a service now. If you'd phoned they would have told you to schedule an appointment," the man said.

"I'll just be here on the steps," Frank said.

"Fine. Sure, sure," the man with the nametag said, and went into the house for a while before returning with the box and a clipboard.

Name: *Frank Evans*. Relationship: *Son*. Date: *July 30, '02.*

Frank traded the clipboard for the cardboard package and thanked the man. Behind him a woman carefully wiped mascara from her eyes, and he apologized to her as he descended the stairs.

It wasn't a hot day, but the sun had filled the car. His father in the box on the leather seat reminded Frank of the smell of a barn's baked dirt floor. Sweat formed on his nose and brow, but he didn't roll the windows down.

AT home, Frank slid the box onto the hall table and noticed Debra on the back patio, squinting at a pair of squirrels racing around the closest tree.

"I never sit out here," she said. "It's cold in winter, hot in summer. Spring and autumn aren't so bad, yet I never sit out here."

The patio was decorated with stones and shells, takeaways from beach trips. Wicker chairs, a loveseat, the cushions covered with a thick fabric the color of sand. In this unusual setting, wearing a pink satin robe, with her hair uncombed, she looked as if she could be on holiday.

"Did you want siblings?" she asked.

Frank sat in the chair across from his mother.

"What is this about?"

"I said to myself, when you were a boy, I wanted another. A brother or sister for you. Your dad, he didn't. Another baby for me."

"I didn't need a sibling," Frank said. "I had my schoolmates."

"I said to myself, if anything ever happened to your dad, I would find a way to have another. Too late now." She twisted the button of the pillow on her lap. "I'm depraved."

"Don't try to have a baby," Frank said.

"Oh, I won't," she said.

Frank had always felt his parents crushing in, as if the family were an inverted pyramid, the top two corners drawing down. They watched him as if they had no place else to look, because there wasn't anything else—including each other—that caught their attention. As two points, they were not as attracted to each other as they were to Frank. But his mother was worse, her frenetic need, which he eventually put words to and pulled away from.

"I don't know what I'll do," she complained.

"I'm making tea," Frank said.

She lay against a pillow and, like a child, and lifted her feet onto the shoulder of the chair. "I don't want to think about it."

"Then don't."

As Frank passed back into the house, he realized how warm and like the car the patio was, the natural heat a comfort. Take everything else away, just leave us the sun.

D E B R A mailed Frank the check. It was his due for being the son of a dead son of a dead man. More than enough. It was a bank check. Not a personal check. It didn't matter if he deposited it. She wouldn't get a message about his independence. She wouldn't learn anything new about him. She was his lost mother in her mahogany-lined study thinking of a new hobby. Horses, rowing, tennis. So, he deposited the check.

Now, morning brought a crisp chill and Frank wasn't going to classes, his prospects limited. He'd interviewed for a job copyediting in the basement of a State Street tower, a job he didn't want. Another, as the reelection campaign assistant to a city councilman, a man who hid his face behind a beard, who looked as corrupt as he just might be. Frank had to find something soon; Bostonians got their business in order before the holidays.

His university ID still valid, he hurried to the theatre district for student rush tickets to the ballet, Firebird Suite, performed by a Russian troupe, as it should be. The line wasn't long, but it was thick with what he assumed were student dancers from the downtown performing arts programs, smoking and laughing. Frank was standing with his hands in his pockets, examining the advertisements on the wall, when a woman broke from her crowd and knocked into him. A red feather had fallen from her hair and she apologized as she knelt to pick it up. Sliding it back into her barrette she said, "I didn't scuff you up, did I?"

"It's fine," he said as he reset his gaze.

"I hope we can get in," she said.

"I'm sure we will. It's Sunday morning, isn't it? Church hasn't let out yet."

She laughed and turned back to her friends.

As the line moved, Frank listened. Harmless gossip about celebrities and plots of movies he wasn't planning to see. Teasing, lots of teasing.

The girls all got their tickets cheap and so did Frank. As he pocketed his, he found himself again behind the group, this time at the crosswalk. The girl noticed him and said, "We're going for coffee to wait for the show. Want to join?"

They stood at the intersection, reds and greens.

"My name is Lynn, but go ahead and call me Feather Head. They do," she said, indicating her friends.

At the time, Frank didn't think much of dancers, what he knew of them, the way they never knew the composers' names and backgrounds, the cracking and popping of their joints, the starved caves of their bellies. They reminded him of Carolyn. Their ambition, which wiped everything else out.

At the diner he sat on the edge, next to Lynn. Across from him sat a lesbian couple, new lesbians he thought, from small towns, kissing for show. Lynn explained quietly to him that these were her A.A. friends. She wasn't supposed to tell him that, she said, but she thought he had a right to know.

"You're not dancers?"

"They are," she said, pointing to the four at the other end of the table. "Not real dancers. Wannabes."

"What are you then?" Frank asked.

"A feather head. Nothing really. A wine baby. And what about you."

"It's funny. I'm nothing too."

"You're British though."

"I'm that."

It was comforting to sit in a large and happy group in the center of a warm and busy diner, the scent of salty eggs and warm maple syrup comingling. Frank had read somewhere that happiness exists only in the moments before you're aware of its existence. Everything after that is pure nostalgia.

He hoped someone from school—a student or instructor—would walk by and see him sitting beside a woman with the nerve to wear a feather in her hair. The red decoration contrasted with a blue scoop-neck dress, which fit tightly over her round shoulders. She wore nearly no makeup, her eyes showing a lack of sleep, and her lips a bit of thirst, too much coffee. From time to time she laughed spastically, but he could imagine how she showed one face here with her friends, and another, one he hadn't yet seen, elsewhere. He wanted badly to see both.

They separated in the lobby under the gild and light. Three sets of red stairs leading to the orchestra, two staircases leading to the balcony. Left, right, center.

Before Frank found his seat, he stopped momentarily at the balcony rail to look into the pit. Shining flutes and trombones, two tall oboes, a harp, horns and a piano. Always, instruments reminded him of his first failures in life, to practice this or that enough to play a tune for his mother's visiting guests.

As the composer and musicians settled in, Frank went to his seat, four rows behind Lynn and her friends. Alone again, between two empty seats, Frank felt the lights coming down, a shadow pulling over him. The stage lights illuminated Lynn's face. The way she chewed her gum, she might be eight years old at the theatre for the first time.

Though he was familiar with the Russian folk tale of the firebird, Frank still squinted at the program book. The strings and trombone set the scene for the enchanted garden, low and snarling dangers in the dark soon interrupted by the light and eerie sound of the firebird's wings. As the prince chased the bird through the fog Frank noticed Lynn apologetically approaching him, awkwardly passing by others' knees and bags. "Do you mind?" she whispered. He took his coat from the seat and motioned for her to sit. The firebird escaped.

Down on stage the captive princesses danced gently to the oboe over harp and the prince fell in love. Ballet was special. The distinct suspension of reality enabled by stage and song, the precise beauty of highly trained bodies, and the way, if you looked very closely, no character could possibly be a minor one.

Lynn uncrossed her legs, brought her hand to her chest as if to contain something wanting out. Frank did not know how to show her she had not made a mistake. He let his hand hover over her knee, bare without nylons, and knobby. Lynn mouthed, "I'm sorry." Already, she'd said it twice.

Frank was energized by the brassy dance of the king: the syncopations, the way the demon and his minions were made by the firebird to dance till they collapsed. Soon enough the prince destroyed the buried egg and with it the horrible king's soul. Finally came the melodic and folksy end. Bells tolling goodbye.

The whole time, he'd been thinking about a video he'd seen of Stravinsky conducting. How struck he'd been by the composer's generous contact with the musicians, the openness of his eyes and hands both to the give and take of the experience. As the lights came back up, Frank turned toward Lynn: "I hope you don't mind walking."

Lynn said, "I have to apologize. I'm a little out of control." The third.

"One thing about American girls," Frank said. "You're always sorry." He could tell, just by saying so, that he'd made her sorry again, and he was glad because he was sorry too. He was sorry all the time.

AT first glance, Lynn's apartment, her bedroom in particular, didn't reveal very much about her. Mute walls and woodwork that the landlord was no doubt happy she didn't have the desire to paint. The sparseness of the apartment might indicate to some people that she hadn't lived there long. But Lynn told Frank she'd been there nearly two years. In her bedroom, she pinned the sort of posters found in a college dormitory. *The Scream. The Kiss.* Kurt Cobain cradling his guitar and smoking a cigarette. She did not have an overabundance of shoes in her closet. Nor did she have a plentitude of jackets, but they were color-coded, which was the subtle mark of how she was gripped. But all Frank noticed was a blue scarf draped over the lamp by her bedside and Lynn, otherworldly in the dark, her nipples like black sea stones.

In bed, Lynn was both careless and unwilling, a slight and uncertain body that seemed close yet distant. Once muscular and pushy, leading with her hands and guiding with her pelvis, then a limp heap staring at the ceiling fan. He'd seen the gold-stenciled design too, thin decoration painted along the veneer, connecting at the blade's edge. A person has an internal life to which they must remain connected. He knew that much.

This time, Lynn feigned sleep as he draped his arm over her hip: rubbing, rubbing, rubbing. Then, snap, she became eager and hungry with her mouth. Afterwards, she coughed and tapped her hand gently against her chest. She coughed shallowly.

"Pitter pat," she said.

Frank waited. "Feel better?"

She coughed again. "You know what it feels like? It feels like double-fisted knocking on a door, but not by one person, by at least ten. Ever feel it? You have anything wrong with you? Doubt you do."

Frank considered the question. "Health-wise?" No, not health-wise. Not really. Otherwise, yes. Many things wrong with him. *Misfit, bore, failure.* Intuitively, he quested to find the person whose own wrongness would counterbalance his, without whom he would always remain off-kilter, as would that other person. Two wrongs make a right was what his impulse implied.

Lynn was sidetracked. She picked up a glass of water from her bureau and wiped the circle of moisture from the surface. "Mr. Death is gone, I guess."

"That's good."

She dressed in a cotton tank and pair of briefs, leaving her sweatpants on the floor. She said, "You shouldn't get dressed either."

"I should stay like this?"

"You have to," she said. "I don't see a lot of naked men."

"Shouldn't we do something?" Frank asked. "Go out. Eat a meal."

"Maybe we should. But, look, it's nine. Superstition dictates: if I leave now, that's eight drinks. If we stay in till midnight, I drink one."

"If we don't go anywhere..."

"I get to be 'off again.' Much more preferable than 'on again,' in case you're wondering."

Frank knew three recipes that might impress Lynn. He could bake a lemon-stuffed chicken in such a way that it kept its moisture. His grandmother had taught him to fry fish with a cast-iron skillet. He also remembered how to make his mother's steak and kidney pie, along with the crusts.

"I'm hungry," she said. "But don't look in my kitchen. It's embarrassing."

Frank looked. Under the oven, she had exactly two pots. In the refrigerator, two limes and a bottle of grape juice. In the cabinet, a box of rice noodles and a bottle of peanut oil.

"You're not really much of a cook."

"I intend to be," she said. "I like salty foods. And umami. Someone told me about that once. You can teach me to cook. That will be one of the things we do together."

Swelling with confidence, Frank began to prepare the meal. They sat face-to-face in the living room and twirled the noodles with their forks. Outside, cars steamed in the rain, the bus groaned to a stop in a puddle. Lynn pretended her fork was an airplane and Frank a toddler. "Around and around and around and around and around. Open your hangar!" Frank laughed. Maybe there were pictures of his mother feeding him this way, but he didn't remember seeing them.

Frank learned that after Lynn had graduated with honors from BU, her boyfriend had moved cross-country for business school. With everyone she'd ever been close—her family included—she'd "lost touch." Frank had *lost touch* too, or tried to, and left it at that.

Lynn brought their plates to the kitchen and rinsed them. She also did their goblets.

"What's that?" Frank asked as she shook pills into her palm.

"Just a little cheat. It makes me violently ill when I drink. It's the weak way of doing sobriety."

"I don't see what's wrong with it."

"Not yet," she crooned in the playful way of a child mocking. "Not yet."

NOW Frank relaxed into the languid passage of days with books, old books by dead authors, and the fresh and welcome concern provoked by knowing Lynn. As a gift one afternoon, Frank brought her a pumpkin. She responded quickly to the buzzer, though it seemed as if he'd woken her.

"Surprise," she said.

"It was two-for-one," he explained, passing her the pumpkin.

He followed her up two flights of stairs, past the cozy entryways of her neighbors, a pair of shoes for each. He visited her apartment so infrequently, every detail held some significance.

Inside, she said, "Can I get you anything?"

"Don't be like that," he said. "I hate it when you act like I'm company."

"Let me just do a few things," she said. "Be right back."

Apple cores and lemon rind littered the sink. One goblet, cleaned and upside down, sat on the counter. He ran water and poured himself a glass and sorted through the mail. Among other business, he found three greeting cards stamped in Eugene, Oregon. These, he'd learned in their quiet, middle-of-the-night conversation, were from Lynn's mother Sally. "You don't open the letters she writes you," he observed.

As she said, "I need to move again. Sally consulted the stars and found me." He noticed the recycling bin overflowing with boxed wine, red. He remembered she'd admitted not knowing one grape from another, just drinking the fermented juice. The very thought of it made him taste the bitter pulp of chewed grape seed. It tasted like disappointment. Disappointment and apprehension.

"I guess you had a party," he decided to say.

"Excuse me?"

"You know this is second-rate fruit, factory-pulped."

She'd brushed her hair, pinched her cheeks to bring on a blush. Seeing him in the kitchen she said, "I don't know what you're talking about."

"What about your pills and your friends?" he said.

"What are you accusing me of?"

"It's pretty clear."

"Look, I don't know what you want me to say. I wasn't expecting you."

He imagined what might have happened, had he come with a warning. The greeting altogether different. Maybe the scent of perfume as he followed her up the stairs. Surely, an empty recycling bin. He'd pass her the pumpkin and she'd place it on the table. Outside, leaves would whirl. Frank made to leave.

"I don't mean it like that." He could see that she wanted to talk away the trouble. "It's my mother. She's harassing me. These letters. She wants me to move back there, you know. This and that. I think she's losing her mind, actually."

"That's a lot of empty boxes," he observed, and immediately wished he hadn't.

"Right. I see. You think I had a man here. Men."

"Stop and think about this," Frank said. "Think about what I'm saying."

Lynn wiped the sink and ran the garbage disposal. When the rush of sound ceased, she said, "I give up."

"Me too," he said and shut the door behind him. But, in the hall, he realized he wouldn't take the stairs. Instead, he leaned against the doorframe and counted the drop-ceiling panels, the water-stained tiles made to look like stucco. He counted fifteen and thought of her fingertips tapping her chest, her clavicles rising out of her torso like the round peaks of a heart shape. He thought of the black and coiled hair of the triangle at the heart's base. Then he knocked again on the door. She opened so quickly he realized she'd also not moved.

At the threshold they pressed against each other trying to find a solution through the embrace. Some people, like Frank, rolled their hurt into a ball tight in their fists, waking in the cold morning with cramped hands, coming to feel tight and arthritic, all the pain having made its way inside, where it remained. Not Lynn when she was "on again." Lynn was the kind of person whose pain was loose, streaming all over her, washing her away or drowning her, as if she were one of those lonely Massachusetts towns, a sun-kissed and bucolic valley turned wet, forever sunk.

THOUGH Frank spent most nights at Lynn's, he'd made a habit of returning to his own apartment on Thursdays. If he did not go back his car collected tickets and dust choked his plants. Also, he needed this time to return his mother's telephone calls. She'd use his voicemail to describe the heartbreaking freedom from marriage she now had. Something in her unblocked, she was taking up competitive swimming.

He dreaded the calls. The inevitable disintegration of niceties. First her singsong questions about the weather, a summary of her best wishes, but then Debra could not resist talking about the money: "Only a wastrel could find himself penniless, if he had what you have. Watch yourself."

Once, Frank had countered her, reminding her whose money it was now. Unable to let it pass, she'd called him a "beastly brat." Frank should not have laughed, but he did.

So, when Debra said, "I hope you've invested it," Frank said that he had.

As this call cycled to an end, Debra said she'd recently begun grief counseling. "Belatedly, I'm sure you feel." Frank listened as she explained how she'd come to believe she could overcome her fear of losing him, her son. She was to end their conversations by saying, "I love you to pieces, Frankie." Frank imagined she'd practiced, in front of her mirror or the shop windows she passed on her evening walk.

"I realize that."

"Do you feel the same?" she asked.

"Of course, of course."

When Frank was alone in his apartment he kept it quiet except for his symphony recordings played low. He'd collected a number of books, many he'd brought home solely for their aesthetic qualities, red and brown cloth covers, gold gilt. And he scanned the texts until what he read became distorted by what was happening within his mind—a long-ago dream turned vivid and palpable.

From the street, Lynn rang the buzzer. Her persistence indicated that instead of thinking he did not hear, she thought he *would* not hear, did not want to hear. Frank turned on the light and met her at the front door. By the way she could not easily balance, Frank felt sorry enough for her, and he could see that the left knee of her stockings was ripped.

Inside, she sat below the reading lamp, rooting through

her bag. He could hear the glass clanking, triplet pints of vodka. She pulled one out and uncapped it. In that light, she seemed younger than her years, clean and clear.

"So, what have you been doing?" she asked.

"You always ask me the same question I am thinking of asking you."

"Very funny. Serendipity."

Frank wanted to think that her words indicated something: togetherness, alertness. He sat beside her and she pulled his hand to her knee, pushed it inside the ripped stocking. She said, "I used to love this. Whenever I got a tear in my tights, I'd sit quietly, stop drawing attention to myself, and rip them open. My mother wasn't too happy. She would have dabbed nail polish to stop the run."

Underneath the taut nylon, her knee felt like an egg, a smooth bump. Lynn capped the bottle and let it drop beside her. The tights tugged and ripped as his hand followed its impulse. He brought her to the couch. She smelled like a dark and smoky pub at the end of a very long night, the scent of pleasant exhaustion. When he closed his eyes the feel of her clothes summoned a different era, a velvet coat, the cords and tassels of her scarf, the silk undershirt. A time when everything was agreeable. But her face against his cheek felt hot and cold in zones, a reminder that sometimes Frank too experienced bright and dark spots. He opened his eyes to see hers closing, the unnatural glow of her whites shot through with blood vessels. He brought her loose arm from where it was hanging to rest gently over her gaunt hip. He couldn't help, in times like this, thinking of Carolyn, of the limitless idealism of Carolyn.

BABY, baby, baby. Not just any baby. Lynn's unlucky baby. Winter was made for pregnancy. Long days in the nest. Frank entered Lynn's apartment, which was starting to feel like his as well. To go to the bank earlier that day, to find out how to add the baby's name to his accounts, he'd worn his suit. It was an old habit to dress-up for banking, a custom of his dad's. You dress for banking because it is business, and business requires formality. And so Frank had found and pressed the suit he'd worn to his dad's funeral and taken the rail downtown. Like a businessman. Except for the humbling fact that Frank hadn't worked for the inheritance, unless being his father's son counted as work.

Now he was eager to ease Lynn's concerns: about their baby's clothes and bottles, schooling, and future. He was prepared to accept the particulars of mortality, but he was also already committed to protecting his child.

A salad wilted on the counter beside an empty bag of croutons. Lynn hadn't eaten anything other than bread—fresh or toasted—in weeks. He loosened his tie, and knocked on her bedroom door, but didn't wait for her reply. In bed, Lynn was holding her nose and breathing through her mouth.

Frank laughed.

"The neighbors are doing some sort of sacrificial roast," she indicated to the courtyard below. "I might throw up our baby."

Frank went to the window and saw three men in parkas poking at a lamb on a spit, white smoke spreading over the dirty snow banks and into the alley. "I'll turn on the fan," he said. "Do you want me to rub your shoulders? Are you tired?"

"Good luck to you if you think you can help me fall asleep."

Frank sat beside her on the bed and rubbed her legs under the blanket. Closer now, he smelled it, and pulled back.

"Done?" she said, and he could tell by the way she moved so easily to anger, to such loose and ineffective anger, that she'd been drinking.

He said, "This isn't the sixties, you know."

"What?"

"I'm not stupid," he said.

"What?"

Frank could tell that Lynn was ready to admit it. "I can't believe I have to tell you this."

"Well, I can't believe I have to tell you that in Europe the standards are completely different," she said and toed into her shoes, tipping into the space between the bed and the closet.

"You're going to leave," he observed.

She steadied herself and said, "I'm going to the market." She meant the corner store on the other side of Tremont Street, which he could see from the front hall window. "Be right back," she said.

He noticed the tidy bulge pushing out from inside her sweater as she moved to the hall. He listened to her sniffling, zipping her boots, dressing for the cold. Then the quiet creaking of the steps and the front door swinging shut. She may have been pregnant, but she was light. Barely there.

When he knew she was gone, he went to watch her enter the market, then exit shortly after with a box of wine hanging from each arm. Tipping, tipping, until she found her balance. It was winter. She could wear a thick black jacket, hat, and scarf, and be anyone on the street, just a lady throwing a party. He knew otherwise. He knew.

Frank finally took of his suit coat and lay it on the arm of the chair. Lynn's couch felt like a comfortable trap, and he sunk in, thinking now of the hasty and crushing depression that comes from not being able to give up. Thought of her complaints of pungent urine, heartburn, ripping aches in her groin that came without warning. He looked at the ceiling lights which had turned into a spread of opals, because with some frustration, Frank nearly cried.

He waited on the couch until she returned from the market, had been to her kitchen, pulled her goblet down, and splashed the liquid in. Sitting beside him, she said, "My mother used to call me 'The Ruiner.' Get used to it."

I F Frank didn't clean her apartment, answer the phone, or check for mail, nobody would. So he took Lynn's messages, made the assurances that she'd call back, and eventually the admission that, no, she probably would not. Two of the women he'd met at the ballet—wannabes, if he remembered correctly—knocked one morning. Lynn hid in the closet.

"Tell them I'm gone."

"Gone where," he'd asked.

"Just gone."

Frank opened the checks from the state, shuffled through the envelopes, and as instructed, placed the letters from her mother unopened in a drawer in the kitchen. "I can't handle Sally right now," she'd offered as an excuse.

Frank knew he should be happier, and so should Lynn. That other people in their situation, expecting, felt optimistic.

Then it was Christmas and gifts arrived. Stuffed zoo animals collected at the foot of a tiny plastic tree. Lynn had turned a corner of the living room, near the window, into a nursery. Debra sent a crib and rocker. European, antique. Solid reminders that this had all been done by someone else before. He displayed his mother's card, signed *With Love*, on the bookshelf above the crib. Hand-knit blankets. Everything satin or soft, everything white and smelling so good.

For the holiday Frank had brought Lynn a copy of *Gone With the Wind*, a heavy book she'd recently begun to recollect passages from, as if the hormones opened her mind to recalling childhood pleasures.

During dinner, Lynn had given Frank his gift, their tickets to The Firebird framed side by side. "You'll see. I save everything. I always remember. I'm like an elephant," she said. "I never forget."

As the sun set to the left over the Charles River and lighted the CITGO sign, Frank snapped on the tree's lights. He'd always enjoyed the twinkling in the dark, the nostalgia.

With the house in order, and Lynn spent, Frank easily and quietly followed his thoughts. Thoughts about his child, not his baby, because he knew they don't stay babies for long. No, soon enough they are strangers, guests in your world, and it's up to you to make them feel at home. He played through the scenarios of his child in the future. If she were a girl, she would be embarrassed by her mother, constantly re-braiding thick dark hair, wearing eyeliner at a young age. If he were a boy, he would never stop believing that she would one day stop. He would sleep beside her in her bed. He would slosh the wine into the toilet. In one scenario, Lynn was sober and, together, the three lived in a small house on a woodsy property. In their home, they recreated a simpler time. The sun warmed them.

In the hours before her labor progressed, Lynn established herself on the couch with her book, turning the pages, rubbing her stomach. She said she couldn't bear to watch Scarlett drink. She agreed; it was crass. She swore she'd make it thirty days, ninety days, forever. The sun had set and Frank sat by, listening to the traffic. The city would wake soon, the groundcover between brownstones perking up, the magnolia buds thickening.

FRANK wondered if it was considered a true disappearance if you had an idea of where the person went. Probably not. Lynn had been gone more than eight hours, the better part of the afternoon and all night. When she got home, she was ruined and apologetic.

She lifted her jaundiced daughter from her crib while Frank stood by like a fireman with a net, ready to catch a falling child. Only, he was hardly trained, desperate and unsure. He held in his hand the bottle and the cloth, and said to her, "Sit."

"Yes sir."

"Who have you been with?" He reached for her arm.

"Not that you care," she said, pivoting into the table and almost dropping Lettie. A pause. Then wailing.

Frank shushed his daughter by repeating her name and bringing her to his chest.

Pacing by the window, Lynn said, "Lots of people in this city. People you know. People you meet. She's fine. She's fine."

"I don't think so," Frank said, patting Lettie's back.

"You just sit there and judge me."

They would argue like this, and he would hear the bolt of

the front door slide into place, as if she thought that by locking it, Lynn could keep Frank from following.

In her black state Lynn made strange comments about oranges and convertibles, asserted her love, fierce as it was, and her loathing, just as fierce. He was a man not wanted, then wanted. This was the push and pull of loving and living with Lynn.

The trouble escalated.

Dry vomit stained her cuffs so that he could imagine her wiping her mouth somewhere in the dark. She turned up the radio and danced like a cartoon set to reverse. Graceless, she fell reaching for a pint from her bag and hit her head against the speaker, blood riding down her nose and off her chin. She developed unusual bruises in hard-to-find places. She fell asleep in the shower; might as well "drown in the flow," she insisted when he roused her.

Debra would phone, explaining that London was lonely without Dad. Didn't Frank consider her feelings? Wouldn't they visit? She was going to explode—just explode!—if she didn't get to enjoy Lettie's infancy. Frank begged her off with excuses: the spring storms, a car seat that could not be gate-checked, colic on an overseas flight. Finally, they'd argue and ring off. His mother didn't ask about Lynn. Had perhaps forgotten.

Frank would bundle the baby and take her to the still-empty reflecting pool, to muddy Copley Plaza, to the library, telling her the story of the public garden that was filling in green with weeping willows, red roses, and half a dozen swan boats moving under the bridge and around the pool.

He thought of Lynn naked with other men. Bone skinny. He knew how her body responded to him, but how would it respond to another man in another situation? Would it respond at all? Did she arch or bend? Did she accidentally moan, even if the man was repugnant? Did he cleanse first or at all? Did these things happen in wet alleys or posh hotels? The concrete steps to a basement? In a small car with a rusted-out carriage?

Then, in the early morning, the telephone rang. A man identifying himself as a police officer asked if Frank knew Lynn, a slight and dark-haired alcoholic, a regular—at least recently—at the shelter on Apollo Avenue in Dorchester, who had been found with a lacerated head, beaten, wandering in and out of consciousness, in and out of mortal pain on Melnea Cass Boulevard. Someone's boot was badly stained. Someone felt responsible. Maybe someone was having a flashback, a memory of pivotal importance. In any case, someone called. Though no one stood by. Not the person with the bloody boot. That someone, or some people, rambled quietly into the night and left Lynn to seep into the glass and gravel. She'd been taken to Massachusetts General Hospital, Emergency, ICU.

Frank waited for morning, for Lettie's first whimper.

FRANK marked time by Lettie's feedings. Another four hours, he thought, accepting a warm bottle from another generous nurse. The foggy ventilator breathed by the bed where Lynn lay intubated, catheterized, heavily sedated. Now Frank split his time between two places he did not want to be, a hostage, personal witness to the passage of waste and pharmaceuticals, air, in and out of Lynn.

Another nurse unwrapped the wet bandages around Lynn's head. Underneath, she was shaved, and a winding trail of black staples brought together the surgically split purple flesh. The way her right side seemed to have borne the brunt of the beating, he could imagine how she'd shielded the left, terrified and protective. He could see from the rapid activity beneath her eyelids that her mind might remember.

In the chair beside Lynn's bed, Frank had fallen asleep with Lettie in the backpack carrier fastened around his front. When he woke, he instinctively pulled it to cozy her tighter, but he felt nothing, an empty pack. Panicked, he went to the hall and found the nurse pacing and rocking her.

"She was fussing. You were zonked. I hope you don't mind."

"No, no, of course not," Frank said, horrified he could sleep through so much.

"I do think she's got a fever. Might want to get her home."

"Thank you for your help," Frank said, reaching for Lettie, whose face was twisted and red.

Frank met the doctor, a young Fellow, in a conference room. "You're her what—brother, boyfriend?" Clearly, the man was tired and probably underpaid; and he did not want to spend very much time with Frank. Neither did Frank want to spend very much time with the Fellow, who reminded him of how little he'd made of himself. "Partner. Boyfriend," Frank said. The doctor explained that the assault had brought on a bleed, which had consequently brought on a clot, which had required surgery. The Fellow said that the EMTs noted alcohol, its smell. What could Frank say about that? What kind? How much? For how long? Had he ever noticed, while shopping at the supermarket, exploring the museum, or strolling in the garden, the distinct tremors of intense need? Any insomnia? "We're treating for withdrawal," he explained. "We assumed." The Fellow ticked a box on a chart. Any other "negatives?" He said, "What information can you provide about her next of kin, if you're not it?"

"I can get you her mother's address," Frank said.

"Before the anesthesia took for the craniotomy someone did ask her, but she didn't feel like sharing."

"My daughter is sick," Frank said, cradling Lettie's skull with his palm. Whenever he spoke of her, he used the words "my daughter" because no other words gave him such confidence or so clearly demonstrated the strength of his purpose.

"I'm sorry to hear that," said the doctor, who, Frank thought, didn't really understand.

"T H I S will be my last letter to you." The opening repeats in a number of Sally's letters. Frank had taken the pile of envelopes from the drawer and opened them after dark. Lynn's mother's handwriting was blocky, straight and square, as if written by a man, or a child just learning. She wrote about life in a state that balanced its budget by releasing its prisoners, one of whom was a new boyfriend, then another new boyfriend, then a man who was not a boyfriend, but who had once been, whose key still worked in the lock, so he turned the knob and came home. Her mother studied both astrology and psychology. She used phrases like "co-dependent" and "alignment." Frank could not help noticing that Sally felt unloved by her daughter, and that this unlovedness held her back in life. She asked if Lynn still burned desert sage, sweet grass, or juniper. She missed the ancient smell of her daughter.

Frank noted the address. It was one of those that indicated a direction—north, south, east, west—and a number in the thousands, a letter of the alphabet to specify the apartment, everything else about it nondescript. Main Street.

F R A N K dreamed there was a mix-up with the tubes and bags, Lynn breathing shallowly into a mirror he holds under her nose, her cry infantile, strained, endless.

Lettie woke him. His body wanted to empty its bladder first, but he thought differently. She lay on her back in her infant nightgown, fingering the ears of a stuffed bear. She looked more like Lynn. The same anxious wideness in her eyes. The same pale skin. Her forehead felt like therapeutic stone, smooth and boiled hot. He ran the back of his hand over her cheeks, smoothed her gown, and touched every burning finger. Wasn't there any part of her not ill? He switched on the light beside her bed and she quieted as she squinted, rosy cheeks, olive oil eyes, warm wet. A fever needs a family, a mother and a father who wake when called for. He could not tolerate that already in her short life he'd neglected her, even if he was fast asleep, exhausted, numb. Never again.

Frank lifted Lettie from her crib. She smelled like hot piss and milk, her whimpers collapsing onto his shoulder.

He slid the girl into her high chair and her lips spread into a roar. "Fast as I can, fast as I can," he said, as he pulled open the kitchen drawers, slid down the baskets from the shelf, and eventually located the fever-reducing suspension drops.

Carefully he measured and mixed the liquid medicine with milk, the only way he could get her to take it. He carried her back to the living room, switching on the light, and settled in the rocker where he fed her, read to her, sang with her, everything with her. He tried to settle her against his chest with the bottle, pulling her gently toward him; but she arched her back, insisted on looking directly into his eyes, thick black pupils in the dark. She sucked and wheezed. Through her gown, he could feel a mass of fever pimples between her shoulder blades.

When the milk was nearly gone, her eyelids began to slide. She then repositioned, extending her legs on either side of the chair, resting against him, leaning and lifting her head against his chest as if she wasn't sure any of this would work.

While Frank waited for her to fall asleep he listened to her breath, fever rapid but smooth, healthy beneath it all. He thought of how her mother's breath raced too, times she'd overexerted, or been distressed, running or caught. He thought of her mother's skinny and bruised limbs wrapped like so around his trunk. He thought of Lynn the dream, the worst behind her. By morning, Lynn had tugged at her tracheal tube and loosened the catheter. A small amount of blood had stained the sheet, which otherwise smelled like cleaning solvent.

FRANK found the step-down unit on the hospital map and rode the elevator with a young couple. The woman reminded him of Carolyn, the way she stretched so freely, pressing her cheek against her shoulder and resting her arm on her ear. Then the woman yawned in an unflattering way, and the similarity was broken.

He'd worn his daughter in a carrier and as she writhed from sleep, Frank remembered to remove her hood so she could make out the shapes and outlines around her.

The woman said, "How old?"

"Oh, coming up on seventeen weeks."

"She's cute. Does she look more like you or your wife?" The man she was with nudged her. "Oh, I'm sorry. That's a personal question."

"I'm sorry," the man said.

"No, it's okay. I mean, it's hard to say. The eyes and hair, they change."

"Right," said the woman. The door opened and as they exited she said, "Take care of your baby."

"Jesus Christ, Sandy," the man said as the door closed.

The elevator rose and the door opened again. A janitor spread his wash over the corridor. Neither pine nor lemon, but a putrid mixture, like rotting citrus in a pantry drawer. Frank walked on, apologizing, but the man took no note, just passed his mop over the muddy tracks.

Lynn began to stir, her knees bending and extending, bending and extending. Her face turning from left to right. As Frank dropped his things on the windowsill, he noticed the dry-erase board. *Your nurse today is: Your doctor today is: Your lunch today is:* Someone hadn't remembered to fill in the particulars.

Lynn was hoarse, a voice out of a horror movie, and eager too, like the living dead, to touch him. "I dreamed we died. In a crash."

"We're all still here," he said.

"We are," she said. She paused often as if to recollect words, to remember approximate meanings. "We are busy bees."

Living meant a lot. Living was a lot of work. Living *right*. Frank could choose to live wrong. Living wrong was an option for any of them, even the couple in the elevator. Living wrong was exponentially easier than living right. Especially if a person can't recognize the difference.

"Is it true? What they say? Someone wanted to kill me?"

"I don't know," Frank said. "Don't think about that."

"I'm not surprised is all," Lynn said.

A L W A Y S, Lynn's wrist was darkened by fading ink. She used her skin to remember. Telephone numbers, addresses, things she needed to buy. Names. Exclamation marks. But her skin did not always remember; the ink faded. Frank encouraged her to keep a notebook. She tried to carry a mobile phone. She told Frank she'd learned that if it wasn't on her body, attached to her body, indelible, whatever it was simply wasn't. And this was how the skin of her hands and arms came to look like a greasy map with the coordinates determined at random.

On doctor's advice, because she'd refused further hospitalization, she was recuperating at her apartment. She would often ask Frank about the reasons. The reason for her shaven head and bumpy wound. For the constant ache at the base of her neck. She phoned Frank and frantically asked him as much, forgetting too that he visited her every afternoon at three.

"Where's Lettie?"

"With us," he said, referring to his mother, who couldn't have been stopped from heading directly to the airport when she'd learned of the attack. He assumed she'd told the other passengers the story while in transit. While he'd waited for the surgery to end, he thought of his mother leaning back in her airplane seat, breathing recycled air, the salt of a pretzel dissolving on her tongue. Sixteen hours later Deb was setting up a nursery in Frank's spare room. He almost broke down.

"Who's us?" Lynn asked.

"My mother and me."

"Are you saying I've met your mother?"

"I am," Frank said, practicing patience. "Come for dinner."

"My head is broken, broken, broken."

"Come for dinner."

Lynn began to talk about meals she enjoyed, foods she craved, the way her tastes must have somehow been changed by the way her head had thudded on the sidewalk. Frank interrupted her. "Write it down somewhere."

"Write what down?"

"That you're coming for dinner."

"I'll write it on my thumb," Lynn said.

He imagined black ink spreading through the detailed pattern of the tiny triangular cracks of her dry skin.

"Done."

FROM the bird's-eye, circling around the issue, Deb and Lettie are steady in the center, with Lynn skidding around the periphery, and Frank pushing himself to make up the distance between. That kind of motion, that pattern of engagement, and disengagement, is easy to chart, and served as a period of practice and learning.

He'd driven Lynn to have her stitches checked and, after an argument, she'd gotten out of the car and stalked through the parking lot. His engine idled outside a pharmacy where pigeons nested behind the neon sign, dropping oddments of their nest to the sidewalk below. Frank parsed his personal history, considered all of the options closed off to him now, and came to a point of complex and irreversible regret.

Deb said that a holiday would give him perspective, and she gifted him with a pass. "I raised you, didn't I? Clear your mind," his mother urged.

The only place he wanted to go, the only person he wanted to see—was Carolyn. She'd be his prophet, his diviner. And so the period of practice continued.

FRANK hadn't seen Carolyn in five years. He should have looked first at her face, but he didn't because of the way she leaned on a black cane. Its mother of pearl inlay depicted a tangle of vines and blossoms. If left alone, he'd like to pick up the stick and touch it. She invited him inside and hobbled toward the wine rack. Frank leaned against the chipped marble countertop. He knew it had not always been cracked like this. Same with the farmer's sink, the porcelain stain. Maybe, Frank thought, someone else had ruined them—a previous owner, a renter, or the sort of person who would install these kinds of fixtures in a Los Angeles loft apartment. Maybe Carolyn was that person. He had to ask himself the question because *she* had not always been this way either.

She asked if she could take the parka still folded over his

arms. It seemed like embarrassing evidence of his life at home. Carolyn said, "You come here unannounced, but I can still be polite," and suggested he leave his bag by the table. "Though I can't let you in my room. The loo is there," she said, pointing to a closet behind the refrigerator.

"I don't need it," he said.

"Wine?"

"No, thanks."

"Don't tell me you won't take a seat?" The way she spoke was so ordinary, so natural, so incongruous with Frank's own nervous anticipation of what might come next.

"Am I being like that?" he asked.

"I think so."

"Maybe I am. How about tea? You want me to sit here? On this couch?" He meant the white leather one facing the sort of expansive window you only find in a loft apartment, a massive glimpse outside.

Carolyn moved like a three-legged animal, with a lopsided bounce that showed her clear determination. It was instinctual.

"You do well with that. That cane. Is that what it is?"

"It's the deluxe. I mail-ordered it. From a catalogue for old folks. I guess that's what we are now, Frank. Old folks. You used to be a revolutionary. And now you're 'old folk.'" She finished brewing his tea and they sat together on the couch. Outside, across the way, Frank noticed birders watching with binoculars. Carolyn told him about a pair of red-tailed hawks nesting on the roof. She said that if he watched long enough, he'd see one of them. The male was known to swoop into the grass for pigeons and rats. "You can see the hawk's prey like a thrashing blotch in the bird's up-swoop."

"Up-swoop?" he asked.

"You know. As it flies back up. You really are relentless."

"I am. I'm relentless," Frank said. He turned his head right to left, working out a kink. There she was, to the left of him. A million soft lint fibers clinging to her sweater.

Carolyn closed the door behind her, leaving Frank to read the take-out menu of the closest restaurant. She said she had trouble with the straight-backed chairs, the wooden seats. She called them back-breakers. She'd said, "Order take-out," so Frank phoned the restaurant and before leaving, knocked on the door. Carolyn said, "Keys are on the counter." Frank thanked her, said goodbye, but she didn't reply. Alone in the lobby, it almost felt like he hadn't seen her, like he wasn't seeing her, but not like he'd never see her again. The keys in his pocket, he went to the restaurant, and came back carrying something new.

SHE reached for the bag.

"What can I do to help?" he asked.

"You can sit down," she said.

"You don't need something?"

"I may be a cripple, but I'm not a *cripple.* Still, since you insist on being useful, just bring the bag to the table."

Carolyn leaned her cane against the couch cushion and worked to arrange the take-out containers on the table. As they ate, the city lit up one window at a time. She wasn't the sort of person to rush to clean up. Instead, they lounged a while before she said, "Trent can be a real shit. I spend a lot of time pretending I'm somewhere else, with someone else." Shadows moved over her. "Does she know you're here?"

"I know what you mean about Trent," he said. The entire time he had been trying to imagine her dancing, costumed for The Firebird, but all he could visualize was the stretcher backstage. He wished she was thinking of him as the prince, entering the castle against her advice. "Can I ask you a question?"

"As if we're not already talking. You know, though, I don't really want to talk." But Frank knew she did; what she didn't want was for *him* to talk. "You could have asked. Said, 'I'd like to visit.' But you fly out here when I'm in the middle of my life. You already have a baby, you say. I don't mean that you should pity me; just look at me."

"I made a mistake," Frank said.

"You need finality. Closure." Carolyn tapped a cigarette on the table, packing the tobacco till it was tight inside. "I have a dream sometimes. You're at the foot of my parents' stairs, leaning in a corner. The stairs creak, and I go to you. And you switch us around, so that I'm leaning into the corner. And you lift my leg. I'm wearing a skirt. And my leg goes up over your waist. And you unzip. And we do it like that. It got to the point where I was thinking about the dream during the day, during waking life. And, the thing is, I couldn't do it that way now, not standing, not with my body all crooked. I don't mean to sound a certain way. Trent's a shit, but he's my shit." She lit her cigarette and leaned back.

The airport—vacuous Logan Airport—came to mind. The wet tarmac. A headache. Even with the headache, he wished he'd stayed there, looking out of the window at the plane taking off instead of getting into it.

"New York is just a four-hour trip from Boston," she said. "Three years I was there."

Frank had been to the city once. Indeed, he'd taken the four-hour bus trip while his classmates celebrated the Thanksgiving holiday. He'd picked the bus up in Chinatown, Boston, and been dropped off in Chinatown, New York City.

They called it the Chinatown Express. And he'd forgotten his duffel bag in the under-bus storage. Because, not two months earlier, he'd read in the newspaper a ballet review mentioning Carolyn, as he crossed the street into the chilly afternoon, weaving through tourists, he looked for her in the faces of complicated women.

He'd stayed in a sullied walk-up hotel, kicking off the blanket when he found it woven through with the pubic hair of previous guests. He'd eaten three meals in three public venues. Went to the steps of the Public Library. Gotten a headache at Times Square. And still not seen her, not exactly. Then he'd returned to Chinatown the next day to find his duffel bag beneath the desk of the ticketer. He'd drank too much coffee and could hardly sit during the ride home.

"Do you remember the irises at the farm we visited? How they filled the field?" he asked.

"I guess I'm just not nostalgic like that," Carolyn said. "But you are. That's okay, Frank. You can remember it however you want. You can remember me however you want." She relied on the strength of her left side to rise from the couch. She moved to the wall and turned off all the lights but for the low lamp on the table. She said, "You can remember me better than in real life if that's what you want." And she returned to the couch, sitting beside him, instead of opposite. And she took his hand. "And I'll keep having that dream."

ROUTINES, habits, haunts: these were still familiar, and it seemed like Lynn took greater comfort in them than ever before. A month ago Frank would not have imagined her plump, but here she was, fleshy and girlish at his door. She had a certain feminine nervousness that he might have found attractive, but because he smelled wine in her kiss, disappointment rose in his throat, where it would make itself known whenever he tried to swallow.

"I'm Debra," his mother said, extending her hand.

"I believe we've met," Lynn said.

Debra apologized. "Of course. Of course," she said, shaking her head.

Lynn looked at the counter, where a bottle of half-empty seltzer stood tall against an unopened jug of fruit juice. "Nothing," she said.

"Just let me know," Debra said and lifted the lid of a pot to stir.

As Lynn settled at the table she said, "Where's my baby?"

Frank explained that Lettie was napping in the other room. "You can go in," he said.

"No, I'll wait," Lynn said.

Debra told how she packed Lettie into her buggy and walked to the Museum of Fine Arts or the nearby Gardner Museum. They sunbathed at Olmstead Park and visited the shops at Brookline Village. She said she preferred this area to Frank's neighborhood, the grit of which she could not assimilate with.

"You should see where I live," Lynn said.

"It's not so bad," Debra said. "You have a window box at least. Your landlord does something with the property."

Frank watched to see whether Lynn registered the mistake, whether she realized his mother had been to her home, and that she had no memory of the day, but she gave no outward sign. She was practiced.

Debra spooned rice and curried vegetables into their bowls and joined them at the table.

"You two don't resemble each other," Lynn said.

"You don't think?" Debra asked.

"Not really. I wouldn't think you were related. Not if I didn't know."

In the other room, Lettie began to cry. Debra stood. Frank thought about the way his mother was with his daughter. How casual she could be. It gave him pause.

"Let Lynn go," he said.

Lynn declined, turning her head down into her plate.

"Go," Frank said. "Give her a fresh nappy."

Frank finished his meal while his mother washed the dishes.

"You didn't have to be so harsh," Debra said.

"I'm sorry."

"I don't mean to *me*. I mean to *her*."

The soap-scented steam billowed from the sink and disappeared into the air as Debra stacked the pots and utensils in the drying rack. Then, one by one, she dried each and returned it to the cupboards. When she was finished, she used the hand towel to wipe the rack as well as the counter. Frank knew the need for this kind of order; he knew it well.

Frank still sat at the table, listening to Lynn talk to Lettie, the cautious and musical qualities of her voice. Lettie laughed and squealed in response.

In short time, Lynn carried Lettie to the kitchen and passed her to Frank.

"I should eat," she said.

Debra returned to the table, but did not reach for her granddaughter. Instead, she said, "Excuse me, but you smell like booze."

Frank watched Lynn's hand and the spoon moving from bowl to mouth. He tried to make sense of the words and numbers written there. He saw then the phrase "*Dinner With Lct*" on her thumb.

"I'm a lush, you know," Lynn said. "I don't mean to make it sound prettier than it is."

"Lush is kind of a pretty word, isn't it."

"Real beautiful word."

"Still, it's not right." Frank's mother said this as if she didn't have a care in the world, as if she could say anything that came into her mind, as if no one were counting.

Lynn chewed and swallowed. Frank tried to swallow too. In his throat he felt the bulge, the bulge that said, *I'm here. I'm still here.*

LYNN wasn't home. Frank had let himself in and finished a second cup of tea by the time he called Apollo House, the nearest shelter. In recent weeks she'd begun attending A.A. meetings in the narrow conference room behind the security desk. He'd walked with her to the entry, and watched as she showed her ID at the desk and opened her bag for inspection. She'd made friends with a woman running away from her boyfriend, she'd told Frank, and sometimes wanted to linger a while after the meeting ended. Frank recognized the voice of the attendant on the other end of the line. It was the bristly chain-smoker who worked the overnights. "Don't call the main line. Call the pay phone in the lounge. Someone will pick up," the woman said, and gave him the number.

Before, Lynn's apartment had been tidy to the point of empty. The cleanliness implied a certain lack of living, of inhabitance.

Now the place looked neglected in a different way; what possessions she did have were left unwashed in the hall, all of her personal effects in plain sight, lest she forget them. She'd begun to wear a backpack to carry her most important items on her body whenever she left home.

Frank dialed. The phone rang seven times before she picked up.

"Didn't she tell you I was calling?"

"I was waiting for a commercial break."

"I'm here at your apartment."

"I lost track of time. Sorry."

"I'll come pick you up."

"I don't like the idea of that. They might see you."

"I'll send a cab."

Lynn said she'd walk a bit, take the bus if her feet got tired, complaining that the oily macaroni salad they served for lunch at the shelter had settled thickly in her stomach. The way she enunciated the word "oily," the trouble her mouth had closing in on the sound of the "oi," told Frank she'd been drinking.

On Lynn's counter Frank found two "pay rent or quit" notices. One was printed on white paper and dated August. The second was printed on orange paper and dated September. The apartment had never felt like home. It hadn't been his, but he'd spent so much time in it, he should have developed a level of comfort in the space. He sat on the couch and looked out the window, thinking of his infant daughter in the lamplight, rolling on the floor. Already, she could sit upright. Already, the sweet mayhem of memory, the confusion of desire with fact.

Lynn didn't return in one hour. Or three. Frank folded the notices and slid them into his back pocket. On the way down the hall he nosed through a black trash bag with his foot, shuffling pint bottles and Chinese food containers. He closed and locked the door, deciding finally to go find her.

In the rain, a couple of students hurried past. As Frank

opened the door of his truck, he heard one of them say "pop economics" and the other something about "Roth IRA." One's voice was goofy and arrogant, while the other's was merely arrogant. He quickly became confused about which student said what. It was so important to keep traction on life; it was important and hard he realized as the white sneakers and ripped knees made their way down the sidewalk deeper into Roxbury. They'd both be soaked by the time they arrived at their apartments.

Frank passed the orderly and square campuses of the Boston Medical Center and fire department, driving toward Dorchester on Massachusetts Avenue. Tonight, he was grateful for the traffic which enabled him to slowly approach and pass every pedestrian, each woman slanting into the rain, backpack slung over a shoulder. He turned onto Apollo Avenue, noticing the refuse along the curb, so many bodies in doorways. The shelter—a repurposed church—was on his left. The fluorescent light in the lobby blazed through the glass doors and illuminated the men and women smoking outside. Frank pulled over in front of the building. He rolled down the window on the passenger's side and waved over a man, asking him if he knew Lynn, if he knew where she was. The man said he'd seen her, but not in days, and asked Frank if he could spare some change. Frank gave the man the coins in his pocket and asked if he would check with the others. "Sure diddly, Boss." Frank waited while the man returned to the awning and spoke to the others. Momentarily he shook his head and waved Frank away.

The rain was like blood letting from a new wound, steady until pressure is applied, then the drops coming thick and fast. The sound on the roof was so distinct he almost hoped it wouldn't end. A sheet of rain streamed over the windshield, blurring the streetlamps and traffic signals, which swayed lackadaisically on the wires.

In the doorways to restaurants and bars, stylish revelers. In the dark and cold, a huddled body, a pair of them, arguing and gesticulating beneath a shared wool blanket. Frank didn't see Lynn. He'd driven into Dorchester, through the stressed neighborhoods and past the shabby parks. Packs of teenagers staggered across the street in front of him, taking their damn time.

At some point Frank realized he'd stopped looking for Lynn. He wasn't sure what he was trying to find. He scanned the pawn-shop windows, the *Cash for Gold* signs, *Checks Cashed Here*. A crazy-looking man in an orange poncho and plastic construction helmet rode his bike using no hands. On the roof of a narrow white house someone kept their life-sized stuffed Bengal tiger. Inside an ice cream shop, a group of young girls waited for their turn, resting their heads on one another's shoulders, blowing bubbles with their chewing gum.

He drove home. He drove home to his daughter.

UNLIKE the others, Lynn eagerly ate the food. The others grumbled over their boxed potatoes, their jarred gravy, and their dry turkey, stacked gray slabs on pink melamine plates. Frank thought of the proverb "beggars can't be choosers." In the kitchen, volunteers stood over the steamy mash, having portioned at least fifty plates in the first ten minutes of service. Lynn craved the salt more than anything. If Frank brought mixed nuts, she'd clap childishly. She didn't discriminate. She asked for the pork skins they sold at the liquor store.

Dinner was raucous. Once, he'd brought Lettie, but she couldn't tolerate the noise. So because Lynn never asked to see her, Lettie stayed home with Debra. No one fought there. This felt more like a social gathering of extended family. Of course, Frank wasn't included. He moved through the dining room like a ghost. But Lynn wasn't an outsider. The animated and teasing conversation included her, drew her in. When a man with a blond braid and leather biker's jacket reached for and snapped her bra strap, she blushed. Frank saw the way Lynn felt she belonged here, the way she'd felt she belonged with her A.A. friends so many months ago, the same way she'd, for a brief time, felt she belonged with him.

When most people had their plates, the dining room filled to capacity, many using the windowsills as tabletops, a squat and leather-faced man cleared his throat to say Grace: "Dear Lord. Bless us all. Bless the staff of Apollo House. Bless the lost souls out there. Bless the cooks. Raise your glasses to the cooks! Please, bless us all. Amen." They drank from their Styrofoam cups.

When Lynn was finished she wanted to go to the store. She cleared her plate and left it in the pail on the windowsill. Frank waved at the volunteer dishwasher, a twenty-something with Down's whose smile showed undeniable pleasure, satisfaction, the soothing effect of having done a job well.

Outside, they weaved through a thick pack of hard-up but friendly smokers. The angry ones didn't linger. You could see them hobbling away on crutches. Counting change. Talking close in the alley. Making threatening remarks into their phones.

"I don't know how else to say this," Frank said.

"What?" He could see that his preface had shaken her.

"We're leaving town."

"Who is we?"

"Lettie and I."

"You're leaving town."

Lynn quickened her pace. She rounded the corner and ducked into the liquor store. Outside a woman stooped over a shopping cart filled with cans. London had homeless too. In Frank's boyhood it was rumored that one of them—she wore a red hat and matching boots—was actually a wealthy heiress. By the telling of the story, she chose that life.

Lynn passed through the glass sliding door of the store, the backpack making her seem underage. Yet, when you looked more closely you noticed how loosely her features were held together; there was a droop to her general appearance.

"Can we go to the reflecting pool?"

"Are you going to keep that bottle hidden?"

"You doubt my abilities," she said.

They crossed onto Huntington Avenue, navigating the construction and tourists outside the Museum of Fine Arts. In silence, except for the occasional question as to whether they should walk or wait at the curb, they passed an anti-war demonstration on the lawn of Northeastern's main campus, then, farther along, noble-faced musicians lugging instruments in their black cases between Symphony Hall and the New England Conservatory.

The Christian Science Center's pool was one of Frank's favorite places in the city. In summer, children waded and danced under the sprinklers. Tourists in visors stopped to rest on the granite benches. In the evenings, couples came to immerse themselves in the metaphor of the endless reservoir and the beauty of reflection at night. Of the full, round moon rising over that particular church steeple.

Lynn uncapped her pint and drank twice. "Take me with you."

"You want that?"

"You don't want that."

Frank paced in front of the bench.

"You can't take my daughter. You leave me with nothing."

"Do you want money?"

"You offend me."

"What do you want? I don't see how this works."

Lynn pulled her legs up and rocked on the seat. "My head isn't right."

"We're leaving, Lynn."

"Will you send an address? Pictures? Can I ever see you again?"

"I will send pictures."

"Do I see her before you go?" Frank considered briefly before Lynn said, "Forget it. I won't remember anyway." She pulled a pen from her bag and wrote her post-office box number on Frank's forearm. "Pictures," she confirmed.

AT first, he didn't send anything. *Make her suffer*. But eventually it made him buzz and ache to hurt her so willfully. He hated to think of her as an abused shadow under an eave. And so after one year passed, he sent a picture. The image of Lettie with curly wet hair, grinning into the bright sun, her feet bare and dirty. Then, a few months later, he sent another to the same box. He never included a return address, so he never knew for certain that Lynn got them. He hoped she did. He could have sent money orders, but for years he sent what she had asked for: photographs he had printed at the One-Hour Photo while his daughter waited at home busy with the woodpile. He knew, he always knew, that if Lynn had received the first photo, she'd received them all.

IN his dreams, Roxbury at night looked dangerous, the littered parks, the cockiness of the neighborhood's youth. Frank wondered which one of them had brutalized Lynn. If it was someone she'd known or someone she didn't know very well. The boots figured into the dream. And the broken glass sparkling along Melnea Cass Boulevard. To the left and right, wide and desolate gravel lots. A couple of prostitutes bending by a chain-link gate.

Melnea Cass was a long road. You got halfway through and you still had a way to go.

It did not seem that Lynn heard him enter. He found her in the bedroom. She slept where she'd dropped, a crumple by the bureau, cradling a drained pint. Seeing her so, Frank didn't feel tenderness. Instead, anxiety, a dreaded hammer cracking down again, yet still managing to startle him. Not affection. Panic that burned in his chest. Not sureness. But a blowing fear that fractured his perception, the poise that had been his burden. This daisy on the floor was tweaking her sparse petals; this dandelion was blowing her gentlest parts away for a lost wish. Beauty and horror combined in the exquisite moment of loss. Frank slapped his own face. He should try harder. He thought, *I will make you feel love. I will make you feel love.* Frank bent to the floor beside Lynn and picked up the bottle, the formula vessel that remained. *I will make you feel love.* But, no. Frank felt something less easy to define.

LETTIE

LETTIE'S SKULL WAS CRADLED in the lap of the boy with the knife. Three men hovered over her, another pinwheel.

"Miss, your head don't look so good," one said as another lifted her onto a stretcher. "What's your name?"

In the ambulance she was told jokes, one-liners, and the two men took turns checking her vitals. *Doctor! Doctor! I feel like a pair of curtains! . . . Pull yourself together!* "Very funny," Lettie said. Between her legs, blood. Another joke: *Doctor! Doctor! I feel like a bridge! . . . What's come over you?*

At the hospital they wheeled her to the nurses' station where she was given a clipboard and pen. "Can you manage?" a nurse asked. Lettie listened to one of the men relating the facts of where and how she'd been found, his head shaking with insinuation. Even the jokes had not helped her trust them, and her playing along hadn't gone very far.

The papers she was handed reminded her of Frank's employment forms, which sometimes she'd found unmarked, folded in the glove box of his truck. Details, details. *MOTHER: FATHER: ADDRESS:* He never forgot, never made a mistake, always left paperwork blank.

The nurse was brisk and young. She had a fast smile. As

quickly as it lifted it returned to pursed. And she said, "How'd we make out?"

Lettie hadn't written anything. "I don't feel so well." It was true. Hot muscles cramped in her groin. In her chest, she felt acid swell.

"Can you give me your mother's number, so we can notify her? The doctor needs consent."

Lettie looked at the waiting room, seeing young children reading, parents with their heads together.

"I'm sure you know what consent means," she said as she unlocked the stretcher and wheeled Lettie into a corral.

"I don't remember."

"You don't remember what consent means? Or you don't remember your mother's telephone number?"

"I don't know." A lie. Even if there had been a fever, even if her father was right about an illness in her infancy, he was wrong about Lettie's memory. Her memories were exact; but there were things she did not know.

"Fair enough," the nurse said. She handed Lettie a white exam gown with thin pink and blue stripes. "Down to your underwear," she said.

"Put this on?"

"Put it on," she said.

Lettie unfolded the gown, stretched the tiebacks, and caught the sob at the back of her throat.

"Something wrong?"

"Blood," Lettie said.

The nurse clucked and checked her head and neck, pulled each of her arms out and examined them.

"There," Lettie said, indicating.

"For the love of God," the nurse said, and opened a different cabinet. "You could have said something. We have these." She handed Lettie three pairs of gauze underpants with a cushioned crotch. "Use the restroom to change," she said. "Down the hall that way."

Thinking as she walked, she passed two gurneys before reaching the restroom. Inside, it was dark. She touched the sticky switches. The first turned on the vanity lights. The second the ventilator. The third the overhead fluorescent strip, which flickered briefly before becoming static.

The toilet gleamed white. She looked for a valve to flush water in and out of the bowl, finding instead the rubbed pedal that made a thunderous whoosh. In Danceland, they caught rain in plastic barrels, roof runoff primarily, and used the gray water to cleanse the toilet bowl and their commodes. They boiled it for bathing and other washing. For drinking water, they pumped from a well in the field. During dry spells or deep freezes, Frank brought home plastic gallon jugs, and Lettie reveled in unraveling the plastic seal. She imagined the largeness of the barrels used to satisfy this large hospital as she undressed and folded her clothes into a tidy stack. Then she pulled one paper towel at a time from the dispenser on the wall; wetting it, rubbing it over her bloodied skin, and rinsing until the fibers began to dissolve.

THE nurse was organizing the contents of the cabinets when Lettie returned. "I left you a bag to put your clothes in," she said.

Lettie was asked to lie on the bed. As she settled, the nurse quickly inserted an IV needle into her left hand, a particular pain she'd never read about. The needle was taped to her hand and the clear tube stretched behind her to the opening of a bag of saline solution. The pole would travel. She itched from the transfer of cool, salty fluid.

"Why are you doing this to me?"

"This is like a long drink of water," the nurse said. "Only it goes in this way, not the way you are used to."

Beneath her was the bleached and starched pillow, at every other angle buttons and lights. She could see things no one else could—the things that if she'd seen a hundred times before, would have come to look like nothing or next to it. It was the first time she'd see a monitor with words and numbers changing on the screen, messages. The first time she'd see a stethoscope, a jar of cotton balls, tongue depressors, hand sanitizer. The first time she'd see a woman, more than one, pacing the hall. How many of them were mothers?

AN officer and doctor woke her. They could be twins, except for the uniforms. The doctor said, "I've looked at your head, which you've hurt, but not badly."

The other said, "If you'll just state a name and number you get your very own ham and cheese, bag of sour cream chips, strawberry sundae party, friends for a visit, afternoon cartoons, whatever you want. Your mom or dad, your aunt, your brother. What's your teacher's name?"

The officer's badge was made of both gold and silver. It said: *Dublin. Police. Detective. Mass.* On it was an image of two farmhouses separated by a field with grazing sheep, the forest and mountains behind it. The forest and mountains where Lettie had been. Where Danceland had been. Where her cat shook and recovered. Where her dad collected copper bits and thrift shop books.

Like her father, Lettie could keep a secret. She felt she had to, to give Frank time to find her, and for the two of them to come to some agreement about Nosey, and, of course, about the future. So the nurse wheeled her up two flights in an elevator and through four sets of fire doors to a room with two beds and two windows overlooking a parking lot. The nurse pulled down the sheets while Lettie looked for Frank's truck in the puzzle of vehicles. If her father loved her, he'd follow, even if he thought she'd behaved badly. That was what Lettie believed. She imagined him searching the cold house, upstairs and downstairs, before opening the porch door. There he'd have stood, scanning the field, checking the treetops, asking Nosey what she knew. Then he'd have begun to explore the forest, helped on his way by animals and ghosts. She wanted him to come into the room from around the corner and say, "So, you see, this is where everybody has been all along." He would accompany her to the cafeteria, point out a man serenading patients from the pavilion, gently hold her hand as she described Nosey's seizures to a doctor, and because she'd shown great courage, he'd talk. He'd talk, talk, talk for once, over a cup of tea in the hospital courtyard. She imagined it. She believed it. And, once he arrived, she wouldn't have to explain anything to anyone; he would. Because she kept her secrets.

IT was a life of nurses. Lettie watched them, egg-shaped, tottering in the hall, bumping into one another, always with the apologies. They ate sandwiches, double-size. The cups they drank from were as long as forearms. They suffered indigestion. It was graceless living. They would have liked their patient to partake, but the food was always too salty. So they fed Lettie as though she were an infant, vegetable purees and breakfast cereal.

They kept the other bed empty. Lettie spent the first four nights on hers, and then tried the other. She did the same with beverages. Orange. Orange. Orange. Orange. Cranberry.

Likewise, she eventually tried each type of cracker stocked in the vending machine, one guarded crescent bite of each.

She did not know how to wash away from home so she showered with the towel wrapped around her, a heavy blanket in case someone should open the door. Eventually, the cleaner asked her to stop soaking them or if she did, for whatever reason, to wring them. After that, she learned to shower uncovered.

She was nearly finished dressing when someone knocked on the door. She'd trained herself to say, "Just a minute" the same way the nurses said it to one another, tone elevated. "Just a minute," everyone in the hospital said. The voice behind the door, an unfamiliar woman's, said, "No rush."

Lettie's loneliness had peaked toward the end of the week, and now it was just a persistent but manageable ache. In the mirror she quickly combed her hair, already cut short by a visiting hairdresser, and twisted it into a clip. After many years wondering exactly what she looked like, she only needed to see herself once to know the answer. After that, she felt she could almost stop looking. She knew what was there. Or she thought she did.

The woman handed her a book. "They said you like to read. This is one I loved."

To the woman she said, "I don't know it." Neither did Lettie know her.

"I always give people a gift first. Then I introduce myself," she said.

It stunned Lettie, just how many people there were in the world, and the frequency with which you met them. Still, when you have a secret, people don't matter to you. All you think about is the secret and whether it is seeping out of you like sweat. She used Lettie's name often as she explained that

Frank had been to town, told the sheriff a story nobody believed until a call came from the hospital. More than by what she said, Lettie was caught off-guard by the repetition of her own name. *Lettie. Lettie. Lettie.* Either Frank used it rarely or this woman used it too much. This wasn't a problem she could solve in the moment.

"So, we know who you are and who you belong to," she said. "Your grandmother will be custodian during this time, at the very least." She explained that the next morning a driver would take her to a school, a "residential" she called it, near her grandmother's home.

Lettie still held the book in her lap. The tips of her fingers worried the edges. On the cover, shadows and ghostly figures, three children and a witch holding a globe, a miniature copy of the world. "If you like that one, look for the others. There is a series." The woman then told Lettie about The Randolph School, the arrangements already made, her peers all from "similar backgrounds." Those words made Lettie apprehensive. *Similar backgrounds.* As if your background defined you; as if you should be grouped with others who were defined by theirs. She knew what this meant for her, and a part of her, the part that did not know very much at all, agreed.

Lettie believed that if her father loved her, he would find her. He'd follow her out of the ghostly woods and leave Danceland behind. Whatever it meant to him, he would value her more. And once he joined her, they'd find a cure for Nosey and live lives like other people. This is what she believed.

EIGHT in their group. Knees pulled up. Twisting hair. Chewing gum. Grabbing a fist of sand and letting it go. The circle expanded and contracted, especially when Lettie held the therapeutic conch and it was her turn to talk, which she did reluctantly. She'd say a word or two, nothing really, and pass the shell to the person beside her. Anyone who was looking would look away. The truth was, she still felt shy speaking to anyone other than her father.

The Randolph School was five miles out of town on the eastern edge of a gated peninsula where the Atlantic towed the shore in and out. The main building was a sprawling Victorian on a hill overlooking the cove. Girls like Lettie slept in the East Wing, wearing more than one pair of panties. It was that common. Other girls bunked elsewhere, hoarding plastic forks and the like. The boys were across campus in what may have once been staff quarters. They did whatever it was that they did.

After session, before class, was open time. Some people watched TV. Others played board games or wrote letters. If it was warm, Lettie's roommate, Amber, and she would walk.

Amber was a competitive and sullen orphan-type, though she indeed had two parents. Her hair had been dyed from blonde to red and back so often that now her two thin braids looked carroty. She bit her lips so that the skin peeled, making the tone of flesh uneven, bloodier here than there. Amber considered herself worse off for two reasons. First, her parents had forsaken her, brought her to the school. Second, her boyfriend had died not even two months prior of leukemia. "We're both a mess," she explained. "But, the difference is, I had a chance."

They walked to the waves, zigzagging toward the driftwood and drying seaweed, clambering over the rocky bits, and eventually settling on the dark sand, some underground mineral giving this particular section a stain.

"I'm in a serious funk," Amber said. "I need to get out of this place. Therapy makes me worse, I swear."

In the distance, a man on a surfboard paddled along the horizon. It had been explained to her, and she remembered somewhat from the initial approach by taxi, that a college campus was located nearby and that there were many comfortable old neighborhoods, homes neatly arranged near one another, separated by woody slices of turf, families living in compartments.

She noticed a hermit crab scrambling, seeming to struggle over the littered beach. Body too squat, legs too rigid. She viewed crab fatalistically, thinking that the closer she got to others, including the crab, the more she understood that her certainties about them were flawed.

If Amber behaved she wasn't staying long, she said. Her parents had already visited twice. Lettie had studied awkwardly in the chair as Amber's father emptied a bag of magazines and candy bars onto the bed. At first, her mother looked like a frightened cat, shoulders lifted and eyes overly wide. Her father went around checking the windowsills and bureau for dust. Both times Amber's parents left promises.

When Amber was discharged she'd return to her life nearly as she left it. When Lettie was released, everything would be new. *Her mother, she never knew. Her father, she knew.*

They treated Lettie with shock. In history, electricity was used. In her case, they used facts; they used truth. A team—a therapist named Charles, a social worker, a psychiatrist—crowded over her file, which was situated as the focal point on the table.

The first story they told was about Danceland, or more accurately, a town of wood and cobblestone structures seized and demolished early in the century, neighbors and friends taken apart, houses, a school, a church burned, bodies unburied to make way for a reservoir which never was let to flood. Lettie lived there with Frank in a remote state-owned ghost town where no one would find them, where not even hikers were allowed except for a once-yearly Historical Society tour. "There are people who would call this cruel, a form of cruelty," Charles said. "Don't you see that?" The end of the first story took place at a courthouse, at a future date.

The next story they told began twelve years earlier and, they figured, was to be continued through therapy. Of course, Carolyn wasn't her mother. Her mother, Lynn, was a transient, a constant in the shelter system on the North Shore. She had very little, yet she drank to excess. She was the definition of the term "polarities." Not to be overlooked, her brain was damaged by a shattering blow in a bad neighborhood when Lettie was a baby. There was no end to this story, Charles told her. It could continue, if she wanted it to. "Just," Charles warned, "do not be disappointed."

Finally, they told about her grandmothers. Lettie pictured them: twin protectors, each mixing a stew. Frank's mother—Debra—paid the bills for The Raldolph School. Lynn's was difficult to reach in the Southwest, but they would keep trying. They hoped Lettie would meet Debra soon because when she was discharged, she would live with her. The phrase repeated in her thoughts the rest of the day. *Live with her.* The thought was scraping a groove in her mind.

Amber didn't mind flip-flopping like a fish washed onto shore, talking about her individual sessions, pumping up the emotion, the fear. To calm herself, she pinched dime-sized bruises under her biceps. "Don't be a victim. I'm not a victim," she'd say.

Lettie could hardly bear to think about her sessions. She'd

been shocked so that the trees and sky were all so bright a fuzzy dimness formed on the periphery, closing in, like the tightening aperture of a camera. She thought she would go on all fours, her head loose, coughing up foam like a seizing cat. It would not help Lettie to pinch and bruise.

Lettie walked. She came to another struggling crab. And another.

LETTIE'S grandmother buzzed in on a fashionable scooter. The woman might be striking in any setting, but in this town she was downright conspicuous. In the first few minutes, she said she no longer believed in cars, the fuel and manufacturing conditions. "Those poor people in Detroit," she said in the same breath as, "Don't call me Grandma. Just Deb. We can always change it later. I used to go by Debra and I changed that too. I'm a believer in transformation."

Charles had brought Lettie to the restaurant and now left them alone, wedging himself into a booth by the bar, waving for his own platter of tempura.

Family resemblance in books usually indicated something, an inheritance, a burden. Deb said she was pleased with Lettie's accent. "A person might think you were raised in Blackheath." Aside from pronunciation, there was also the high and even forehead, the polite nose and pretty lips. Deb said Lettie's hands, even, were of the family. She thought they had a nimble quality, making them good for piano and guitar.

"I know what you're thinking," she said. "You want to know what it is between your mum and me." Lettie was disturbed by the woman's abruptness, and her fondness. As much as she wanted to know more, she'd come to expect the facts to hurt, and she braced herself for the burn. But her grandmother simply said, "She's easy to love and she's so grateful," before moving on to tell how she herself had been living in the States for years, in a cottage on the cove. She went on about all of the things she loved to do. She talked so quickly, and at such length, as if no one had ever listened to her before. Swimming was her sport, she said, and Lettie pictured a red silicone swim cap bobbing under the waves. Large dogs, even if they always smelled like wet, were her favorites. She talked about Frank, of course, when he'd been a boy on his bike and later, a remarkable student. "Your dad is a loving person," she said. "It's his nature. Now that I've seen other men for who they are, I recognize the differences."

"I know that," Lettie said.

"You shouldn't begrudge people. Not for the mistakes they make." She said this quietly, as if she intended for no one else to hear it.

Crisp fried rolls were brought with tangy dipping sauce. Lettie sliced and found green and purple cabbage inside. Deb mixed the bright top layer of her iced tea with the dark bottom, two tones blending. Lettie did the same, tasting at once cream and clove together for the first time.

It must have been important to her that her granddaughter know all of the things she loved. She went on. Long letters sent by post. Hand-forged wide bangles. All forms of cosmetics, the sweet dust in the air for just a moment. A single glass of Pinot Grigio with good company on a summer afternoon.

"One and only one," she said. "People will scrutinize you because of your mum, who you shouldn't begrudge either, when you meet her."

Deb said she loved the States, much more than England,

especially this coast. She loved to see cows eating grass so close to the sea. And the lottery. She didn't play, but she tuned in, and adored the news coverage of winning players, their desperate lives fixed just like that. The evening news: add that to the list.

"You love my mum?" Lettie asked.

"Of course I do."

"I don't know if I will."

"You have to."

"What if I can't?"

"I'd like to take you to see her."

"Where?" Lettie pictured the underside of a bridge, a polluted railroad yard. Things she'd now seen on TV.

"We can go to the shelter."

"Visitors are allowed?"

"Of course. Maybe next week?"

"Okay," she agreed.

The talk of visiting Lynn brought Deb to her recent supervised reunion with Frank at the minimum-security facility in the western part of the state. "I hadn't seen him in more than a decade. I don't know how happy he was to see me. But he misses you bunches," she said, refolding her napkin on the table. No, "bunches" was not a word Lettie and her father would have used. No resemblance in that. As Deb paid the tab a dark shadow passed over the parking lot. They gathered their things and Lettie's case manager followed them toward the door.

Outside, it had begun to pelt, a powerful current rushing from the gutter to cascade over the sidewalk. The raindrops picked up force. The atmosphere spent, tired of keeping the weather liquid, gave in to chilling the molecules as the raindrops formed, a final act of bad humor. Deb opened the door and extended her hand, collecting a handful of bleak but miraculous spheres of hail.

THE telephone in her wing was located in the lounge, which was made up of simple oak furniture with irritating fire-retardant upholstery, and a small television that could only be operated by staff. Other girls might be watching sitcoms or crimping one another's hair on the couch, listening. Staffers would be sitting in the chair by the door, twirling key chains, chattering like they were girls even though everyone knew they weren't. Someone, at least one, but sometimes more than one, was always on Watch. Being watched, that is, to make sure the situation—their life situation—was kept controlled. Whoever was on Watch was to stay to their room where a second or third staffer set up another chair by the door. Knitting was the most dangerous thing you could do while on Watch. Lettie never knit. She never went on Watch. She just observed. Saturday mornings she smelled buttery pancakes, berries boiling in their juice, coffee and hot chocolate. She could hear the cooks in the kitchen cursing the appliances.

Apologizing, Frank said the line for the phone was always long, as if that was the reason he hadn't called.

Amber mouthed, "It's your dad?" and Lettie nodded, stretching the cord to the bench in the hall. Of course, they could still hear, but it felt more private and that mattered.

"Is your cell too small?" Lettie asked.

"I'm not there a lot," he said, explaining that he had a job mowing and weeding the lawn, he was in reading and movie clubs, he went for therapy on Tuesdays and Fridays, he found a friend to play cribbage with. He read a lot.

"I read a lot too," she said. She didn't have much time or privacy, but each evening before sleep she read a few pages from the book given to her before she left the hospital. The prologue explained that the book was based on a 1965 Nobel Prize-winning physics theory of multiple histories developed by Richard Feynman. In the novel, three children meet a witch who shows them that though they remember their past as one continuous journey, each of them has actually traveled along a variety of unconnected paths. The children in the book are looking for their father. Lettie, on the other hand, was looking for her mother. The nurse mustn't have remembered the book very well, or else she'd have been more sensitive.

"That's good," Frank said while, behind him, the bewildered and guttural laughter of men rocked the conversation. In her own lounge, the girls bitched quietly, so as not to be demerited. Over the din, he said, "I have to apologize."

"What?"

He was talking on an old-fashioned pay phone. All of the lapses, the long pauses, had added up and now an operator cut in asking for more money. This, he wasn't prepared for.

"I don't have any more money," he said.

"I know." She'd been twisting a gimp friendship bracelet she'd made for herself, and now the knot was coming loose.

"Have you seen her?"

"I should." She shook the bracelet to her wrist bottom, where, on its own, the thread continued to come undone.

"Do."

The operator interrupted, "The call you have made requires a coin deposit."

"Bring her a bag of pretzels. Or potato chips," he said. "Darling?"

But the operator said, "Goodbye."

It wasn't difficult for Lettie to imagine Frank hanging the phone on the hook and turning, worn out, down the hall. She clearly visualized her father in his new environment, as she might in any environment; he'd gathered so much pain he moved slowly and deliberately, still driven by a vanishing dream.

Later, much later in the day in the cafeteria for dinner, she realized she'd forgotten to ask about Nosey. The gray-blue sky outside the dining room window played various scenes from the cat's life. Past, present, and future. As a kitten, claws undeveloped, her hardscrabble approach up a maple tree and the way she landed perfectly upright. The tense arch of her spine during a seizure. Her leathery nose sometimes wet, sometimes dry. Prowling the cellar holes with other cats, and alone. Dreaming of the field.

IN the third bed, under her sheets, a new girl was panting, but she finished quickly.

Amber and Lettie dressed behind the bureau. Amber whispered, "Not those shoes. These," and pushed her sandals toward Lettie's feet. Then they slid out of the window and ran over the nurtured lawn toward the dark road, passing in and out of the moonlight. When they slowed, Lettie asked Amber if she thought the other girl would tell. Amber said, "Live and let live."

Amber's counselor—his name was Anthony—had given her the directions to his apartment, not a mile from Randolph's campus. She kicked a can. In the distance Lettie heard a boat blow its party horn. She could taste salt. Amber was saying, "We need a word. A safe word. A get-me-out-of-this-situation word."

"I'm sure it will be fine," Lettie said.

"You've never been raped."

"Have you?"

"I know someone who has. It's not exactly a good thing. I wouldn't want that to happen to you."

In their group's therapy circle, the person holding the conch would tell the story of what had happened to her. But the way Lettie's father had kept her life so free of trouble, so confined, she felt like nothing had ever happened to her. If she'd stayed, maybe nothing ever would have. Or maybe she was confusing things.

Lettie said, "Jump."

"Jump?"

"'Jump' is the safe word," she said.

"That's a good one," Amber said, stepping onto a rock and shooting off.

Anthony was sitting on the steps to a wraparound porch, the old Cape rising behind him. In every window, light and people. Amber hugged him and opened the cooler, pulling two bottles. Lettie envied her, making herself right at home.

There they were. Brown and green beer bottles. Lettie had collected the round shards washed up on the shore. Now she'd seen, in cartoons, people suck them until they went inside-out within the glass. And she had this image of her mother drinking too. A needy haze, whatever she looked like, with her belly bloated and hard like Lettie's when she drank too much water too quickly. Amber gave Lettie her first drink and she swallowed the beer like it was soda, paying no attention to the tickle of bubbles in her throat.

They sat on the steps while Anthony smoked a cigarette. A sturdy calico prowled by, coming to rub her ears against Lettie's shins.

"Hello," she said to the cat. "Who are you?"

"That's the neighbor's. Its name is Scoot."

"Hello, Scoot," Lettie said. The suddenness of love is funny. She felt in the moment that she'd trail that cat without end, half expecting it to seize.

"Come inside," Anthony said.

"I'll be right in," Lettie said to them.

"Don't go anywhere," Amber warned.

"I'll be right here," she promised.

The cat had coiled between her legs on the bottom step and began to sleep as Lettie combed its long hair with her fingers. So many pieces of crushed leaves clinging to the soft hair. Inside, Lettie overheard Amber's voice rising, "She'll come in when she wants, *if* she wants." But, quickly, she appeared in the doorway and said, "Bring us a couple of those, why don't you?"

"Fine," Lettie said, running her fingers over the cat's resting body one last time.

Inside, people sat awkwardly, leaning forward or slouched too far back. Lettie recognized a few people from campus. The woman who collected her laundry nodded. It was different, not to see a nametag pinned to her polo.

Amber said, "Why don't you sit over there and talk to Prem."

Prem waved a crutch, his right leg wrapped in a cast and resting on the table. The thickness of his eyebrows gave the impression of maturity and age, though Lettie would not wager a number on it. Amber held hands with Anthony and, together, they went upstairs.

"Don't you want one?" Lettie asked Prem. Based on certain things Amber had said, she'd assumed not only that everyone would want one, but that everyone did have one, even though she knew that some *would* and *did* far too much, like her mother. She was swallowing so fast now, partly to be one of them, partly to know which category she'd fit into, if such a thing could be known in just one pass.

"I don't drink," he said.

"Are you kidding?" she asked him, settling awkwardly on the couch. The others shuffled, repositioned, regrouped, so that eventually Lettie and Prem were alone on the couch. If Prem knew anything about Lettie, he didn't say. He was a fecund storyteller. The way he talked his eyebrows moved, his face screwed up and then undid. He had an overblown sense of things. He found humor in whatever he encountered. And it was funny how she quickly found herself much closer to him on the couch than she'd been at the start, already reaching out to touch his cast, to feel the crisp texture of plaster and cloth. Also funny was how the bottles on the table multiplied around his leg. Lettie thought of the cooler on the steps, how the skinny factory ice must be swimming. Funny, finally, were the multitude of conversations, all different interactions happening at once, everyone alive together.

"I like the way you laugh," he said. His smell was of soap and blooming fruit flower. Lettie felt like she'd never laughed before, and upon realizing it, her mouth turned into a pout she could not control, thick and somehow turned upside down. She nearly moved for another drink, but Prem said, "Let's go for a walk. Don't crack any jokes. I can walk with this," he said, lifting the crutch.

To get her bearings Lettie reached for the wall, but she didn't see Amber. If she'd seen Amber, she might have found a focus other than Prem. Atoms flared, sparkled, and died on the margins. She decided to count. It was a method Charles had recommended during group therapy one jittery afternoon when none of them could get it straight. So, she started counting. She counted the seconds it took Prem to situate himself. 1 – 2 – 3 – 4 – 5. She counted the jumps he took to get on the path to the porch. Ten. She counted the grunts getting out and onto the grass. Seven. The calico skittered from the hostas and prowled behind the house.

They explored the shadows, his crutch scratching the gravel. He told about Anthony coming out of the woods one night covered in ticks. Prem thought he'd tweaked them out, gone to sleep, and the next morning still had to put three matches to Anthony's neck and ears. "Sure as rain, guy comes up with these gigantic red target marks a week later. He got Lyme."

Prem stopped at a bridge, the second and larger one to connect the peninsula to town. "Accounts for how crazy the guy is," he said, sitting on a bench overlooking the water. "Hey, I'll check you later for bugs. Is that what's scaring you?"

"I'm not scared," she said even though she was thinking of the flat and smart ticks dropping from the leaves above them.

"You look pretty scared." He hobbled toward the crumbling concrete wall and said, "Let me see you." He jiggled the back of her tee-shirt and bent before her to tug the pant legs, touching her ankles and finally, bracingly, smoothing the backs of her calves. She lifted onto her toes, thinking of Carolyn Brody Taylor, the woman who should have been her mother, *en pointe*. She returned her weight to her heels and he pulled her hair into a ponytail and wiped her neck. "Bugs don't like you," he said.

The whole time, she'd wanted him to keep talking, so she wouldn't have to. She was worried, once they started to kiss, that he should somehow continue to tell his stories because if the conversation turned to her parents he might mistake what she had to say about them for what she meant for him to know about her. Mercifully, he kissed her, his lips like two roasted turnips: warm, yielding, and sweet. He wrapped her arms around his waist.

Most of the girls in her wing had been abused sexually. Until this, no one had touched Lettie. It confused her that not many of the girls at Randolph believed her.

Prem lay awkwardly, his cast leg on the bench, the other bent and supporting his weight. Lettie rested her head on his shirt, trying to name the scent of him: apple, strawberry, plum, pear.

Amber came out of the woods alone. "You don't do that," she scolded with both hands outstretched, palms up. The stance that said *honest*. "You don't leave. We don't leave each other, ever."

"Sorry," Lettie said.

"You don't know what kind of crap has gone on."

"Yeah, calm down," said Prem.

But it was impossible, because what the drinking had done was make everything more. More, more, more. More love. More hope. More trouble. More sadness. If the night weren't so short, more drinking. More, more, more.

"We're out of here," she said, latching Lettie's arm with hers. But before she let Amber pull her away, Lettie gave Prem his crutch. As Amber tugged her back, he became an outline on the bridge, a silhouette of a man leaning for support. Amber was disappointed in her. She chastised and warned. Eventually, she told Lettie that Anthony was overweight under his shirt. When they returned to campus, the night-awake staff were still sleepily huddled by the TV in the lounge. The girls settled into their beds, but Lettie couldn't sleep. She lay there realizing she hadn't asked Prem about his cast. She hadn't asked him about anything. And she still so wished she could name his scent.

RULES were not difficult for Lettie to follow, but Charles said she needed to "get with the program" in regard to healing. Every day she would hold the therapeutic conch in her hand, a heavy and pink shell with a spiny peak, and shrug.

They used the conch because if you put it to your ear and listened you would hear the place it had once called home; it was a symbol for talk therapy. Also, and this applied directly to Lettie, she'd been told, in Buddhism the conch is used to rouse disciples from the "slumber of ignorance." It is used to call them to care for themselves and for others.

To Lettie, the significance felt forced, and she'd said so. How could one minor object have so much meaning when her whole personal history was composed of questions, vast segments of her knowledge actually untrue? She shielded her eyes from the sun with one hand, held the conch in the other, and said she was happy to know her grandmother, who reminded her of her father. "Everything else is fine." Then she passed the conch.

Despite her generosity, Deb held back. Despite her façade, a lot did not pass over her tongue. Same with Frank. Bundled under his yielding work shirts and beard, so many secrets.

Charles said, "No, Lettie. Hold the conch just one more minute."

The girl beside Lettie handed it back.

"This might sound like a strange question, but do you ever miss Danceland? The place your father called Danceland, I mean."

No girl wants to haul trees the way Lettie did or get a cramped hand from sewing. Of course she did not prefer the cold or ill-fitting clothing, and she would not choose to live again in the cottage. But she missed the irresistible physical influence of her father, his coming and going a rhythm to her heart, and her sick cat, softly returning to composure after a convulsion. She missed the enamel stove the color of butter: cool in summer, radiantly warm in winter. She missed the porch door.

But mostly, she missed certainty. A feeling that what is real is what is right. That the rightness all around her actually included her; that she was right too. The knowledge that there had been a time in history, not distant—a time that might in fact repeat—when men in the town square would whistle their tunes while fine-looking mothers spun on the grass with their children till together everyone reached a euphoric dizziness.

"You know more about me than I ever will, and what you know is next to nothing," she said to Charles.

HER mother followed the shelter rules. The dorm downstairs was for "sicking and sleeping only." On the day Lettie met her, Lynn was "sicking."

Deb had a way of walking as if she simply preferred to be side by side. Sometimes her wide hips and Lettie's would barely make it in a narrow hall and she'd say, "Scooch, scooch," as they turned sideways to pass through. The shelter attendant said, "Watch your step," as they descended into the dorm. He was a rough and pockmarked man who ran his key ring over a box beside the rusting metal door. The box beeped.

"I've actually never been downstairs," Deb said.

The attendant said, "Just look, Deb. Cameras there," he pointed, "and there. And there too."

"Wave!" she said.

Lettie turned toward the sound of a man snoring into his pillow. "Him? He's harmless," the attendant said. "He's good crazy."

Four rows of bunks. Donated and mismatched bedding. An American flag draped over the window. Garbage bags wedged under every base.

The attendant led them to the back, where a sheet separated the large men's dorm from the much smaller women's. He knocked twice loudly, then a third time: "Visitors."

Lynn slept on her cot, a mound under an afghan.

The attendant spoke loudly, Lettie thought harshly: "Visitors."

Deb lifted her finger to her lips to quiet him. "I've got it. Thanks." And the man left. Deb said to Lettie's waking mother, "Remember I told you Lettie was coming? She's here now."

Six cots filled the small light-filled dorm, bedsheets tucked tightly, pillows and rag dolls, perfume, arts and crafts necklaces the colors of the rainbow. Above every bed, wallet-size pictures of boys and girls, children and grandchildren, nieces and nephews. Celluloid.

"Are you sick?" Deb asked.

In Lettie's presence, Lynn's first words, after *everything*, were: "Someone stole my meds." She had a mismatched, sharp and slow way of speaking. Her red and cracked hands shook as she tried to smooth her hair. Beneath her bangs the skin puckered into a scar, which Lettie knew extended behind the head.

"You have a visitor."

"I know," she said. "She's my daughter. You told me. You told me."

Lynn sat in her bed and motioned for Lettie to near her, but the girl didn't move from the entry. Deb had made herself comfortable in a white utility chair beside the door. "Go ahead, go ahead."

To Lettie, Lynn seemed young and—aside from the disfigurement of her forehead—beautiful in a slightly messy and loose way. Her knees, for example, were spread so wide Lettie saw yellow cotton underpants, but her mother's thighs were well-shaped, slender.

"You had a birthday," she said. "If I'd gotten some advance notice, I'd have a gift. Do you like chocolate?"

"Not really," Lettie said. The powerful scent of urine and bleach, combined with the motion of the nod, made her dizzy. A part of her desperately needed to be outside, where she thought she might feel more balanced.

"Did they diddle you on your way in?"

"Of course not," Deb interrupted. "New topic."

"I just don't see how this place stays in business," Lynn said, standing from her bed and tidying the blanket. Her hair was more than one-night's messy. She tilted to one side, like an unsteady candle.

Before the visit Charles had asked what Lettie's concrete goals were for visiting her mother. She'd decided she had two: to find out why Lynn had never looked for her, and to have a photo taken.

"You look healthy. Your father, he ever diddle you while he holed you up?"

Deb interjected, "Lynn, this isn't a joke. New topic."

Lynn said, "He never diddled me very much. I just wondered."

She seized a bumpy drawstring bag from the stand beside her bed. "Do you like jewelry?" she asked. She did not wear an undershirt or bra. Beneath a thin cotton halter, you could see the subtle bounce and sway of her breasts.

"My ears aren't pierced or anything," Lettie said, pinching her lobes as if to check again.

"I have necklaces and bracelets. Take something as a gift. You have a nice voice. You talk like him. Don't mind my hands shaking."

Lettie emptied the contents onto the bed, studying each piece. As she did this Lynn told a story. When she was Lettie's age an older boy invited her on a date. It was almost a joke that he'd even asked, she said, because his hair was sun-streaked and his legs muscular from being a forward on the soccer team, and also because he was an older boy. "He dialed my number by accident, that's how he got to know me. He meant to call my prettier friend, but got me. Maybe he liked what I had to say." She told how she dressed in a white cotton tee-shirt screen-printed with a dense pattern of geometrically constructed sunshines, every one of them with two bright spots for cheeks. "My mother was boozing on the front porch with some boyfriend," she said. "They were watching the clock as the minutes and first hour passed." Lynn said she'd sat on the floor in the hall, with her head in her hands, until the telephone rang past midnight and the boy apologized. He said he didn't realize he'd forgotten her until halfway through the party, when he was too drunk to drive.

"That's sad," Lettie said. "He was kind of a jerk."

"There's a lesson there. I didn't learn anything though."

Deb coughed, as if to indicate and maybe apologize for her presence. "I'm sure you learned a thing or two."

"I never learn. That's the beauty of me," Lynn said, laughing and coughing.

Lettie held up a silver chain with a sea-star pendant. "I like this one."

"It's yours." She lifted her tremoring hands to her chest. "I don't feel good, to be honest."

Deb said, "We'll go, but first Lettie was wondering, can she get a picture done with her mum?"

"I suppose. Have you seen this one?" she asked, pointing to a tiny frame on the table by her cot.

When Lettie reached for the frame, her mother stopped her. "Kiss me? Please kiss me."

Lynn pushed the hair from her face and Lettie leaned toward her mother's cheek, smelling burnt sugar, seeing swarms of blood vessels, and the wound.

"Here," she said, handing her daughter the battered frame. In the picture, Lettie sat with her knees pulled up on Frank's chair by the stove, wearing a long white men's tee-shirt, her lopsided smile showing she'd lost a tooth.

Lettie's memory, time itself, buckled. The feeling of fever crept over her, as she considered her image in the photo. How did Lynn have *that* photo? A baby portrait, maybe. But what was pictured in *this* photo was of her time alone with her father in Danceland.

No, it wasn't until later, much later, that she learned her father had sent the photo, that her father had sent hundreds of photos. That Lynn kept three full albums in the shopping bag beneath her cot; photos she brought with her to therapy and shared with her boyfriends, the special ones. But before these particulars could come to her, in Lettie's first meeting with her mother, Deb snapped the camera just once.

"Stop. Careful. Stop. You'll attract them," Lynn said, backing into the men's dorm.

"Them?" Lettie asked.

Lynn whispered, "Them, them." She pointed to a drain in the tile.

Deb placed her phone in her purse, tilted her chin down, and lifted her eyebrows. "Thank you so much, darling, especially on a day you're not feeling your best."

"A pleasure," Lynn said. "A real pleasure. Bring me a copy of the picture next time." She'd put the frame back in its spot and opened her purse. She took out a cigarette, matches, and a bottle of vodka.

"Outside," Deb said.

"I know the rules," she said, gathering her bag.

The sleeping man was waking as they walked through the dorm. He coughed like he was bringing something up, but nothing came. They passed through the doors, cracked glass reinforced with duct tape and a *NO LOITERING* sign.

On the steps, Lynn reached for Lettie's hand and passed her a quarter. "This one is from the year you were born?"

Lettie looked at the quarter. "Thereabouts," she said.

"It's close though, right?"

A man wearing a bandana around his bald head wrapped his arm around Lynn's shoulder. "This is my girl," Lynn said.

The man said, "Your daughter is a stunner."

To Deb, Lynn said, "Will you talk to them about my meds. Someone, I have an idea who, has stolen my meds."

EXCEPT for the occasional incident on the lawn, a tangle of staff and an out-of-order student, The Randolph School was a quieting setting. Yet after meeting her mother, Lettie rushed even as she lay in her bed, even as she draped herself on the couch, and rested on the toilet. When she thought of her mother, which was unavoidable, and put her finger to her wrist, she felt her pulse skip hurriedly, unnaturally. If she stood, she thought she would fall.

At their weekly meeting, Charles, who smelled in the moment like rubbed eraser, said, "You'll take this pill in the morning. And this pill when you feel something bubbling up."

"How do they work?" she asked, examining the vials.

"We don't know. It's complicated."

She was almost finished reading the book about the children traveling through alternate universes looking for the father they did not know they had. "I'm interested in that kind of thing," Lettie said. The mind. What she couldn't see. What she couldn't know. In strikingly narrow wormholes and what traveled between. In the molecules of a tiny oval pill.

"Some people never realize what they have to say until everyone else who had a say in the matter is silent," he said. "What do you have to say?"

"I don't know. What am I *supposed* to say?" she asked.

"You decide what you have to say. I don't."

"That's true," she said. "I'll take this for the field trip."

"You're going to the mall?" he asked.

"I've never been. Amber says it's something I have to do."

"Amber knows everything, doesn't she?"

"She's been through a lot," Lettie said, swallowing the pill and handing him the vials, which he would later give to the residential staff, who would ultimately be responsible for making sure she took them. Lettie was responsible for so little, just for becoming herself, whoever she was going to be.

Back in their room, Amber was brushing her hair at the window.

"So, he gave you pills? Which ones?"

"I didn't really pay attention," Lettie said.

"Do you feel screwed up right now?" Amber asked.

If she thought about how she felt, she felt pretty bad. If she didn't think about it, it didn't matter. Lettie said, "No, I'm fine. Let's get out of here." She finished brushing her hair and slid a kohl pencil over her eyelids before they joined the other girls in the hall.

THE group dissolved as girls broke into pairs and threesomes. Amber jetted to the discount drugstore, with Lettie following close behind. She gravitated to the cosmetics. The scent Amber sprayed on Lettie's wrist was a combination of skunk and sweet. Amber squirted hers and rubbed. "This reminds me of my boyfriend. It's okay. It's a good thing," she said, referring to the memory of the dead boy.

They had forty-five minutes before they needed to meet the others at the pavilion and return to school. Amber wanted to show Lettie RAGE, a store stocked exclusively with colorful and flimsy clothes for girls. The two mined a plastic tub filled with bras and panties.

"This is ridiculous," Lettie said, holding up a pink thong embroidered with green sequins.

Lettie's father had assembled her Danceland wardrobe with items he'd found at thrift stores and the airport lost-and-found. The contents of the bags smelled like rotted wood. And he wasn't one to notice small tears. Lettie washed and mended, but still she knew that clothes were meant to fit not hang, not cling or roll up. And now Deb brought clothes whenever they met, garments that were clean and of sturdy construction. Soft and colored like the earth: blue, green, brown. Still, Lettie wondered what she would look like if Amber dressed her, or if she dressed herself.

"Maybe I will try some things on," she decided.

"Let's try on wild things."

Amber began to collect garments, draping them over her arm. She scrutinized the tee-shirts and jean jackets on the left wall, then what she called the "throwback" styles collected among the aisles in the middle of the store. They ended on the right wall where the pretty dresses were hung. For every three items Amber selected, Lettie found one. The browsing focused her in a way none of the therapy had; she passed over the fabrics and colors, the patterns and cuts, engrossed.

"Let's go," Amber said, eventually pulling Lettie into the dressing room.

The girl behind the counter waved and they closed the door behind them.

"I don't think we both fit in here," Lettie said.

"How are we going to try all these on if we don't share? You have to maximize your opportunities, Lettie." Amber said things like that: things that didn't make sense, but seemed to come naturally.

They squirmed out of their shirts and jeans and into the fantasy clothes. One shirt had a completely open back. Lettie twisted at the mirror and realized she had a birthmark under her right shoulder blade.

"I didn't know it was there," she commented.

"It looks like the state of California," Amber said. She was wearing a tight white crochet pullover that required a camisole. Beneath it, she was creamy white.

Lettie laughed when she saw herself in a purple faux-leather bodysuit.

"I should take a picture and send it to Prem," Amber said.

His name said aloud made Lettie flush. So often she thought about him—his name and the memory of his solid presence always just under the surface of whatever she actually said and experienced.

Everything was costume until she came to the clothes she'd carefully picked out. Amber was fastening a shiny yellow halter top while Lettie pulled a pink dress with a wide skirt over her head. The dress came with a skinny metallic belt and she'd found a matching pair of flats.

"You look pretty in that," Amber said. "Where did you find those ballerina flats?"

"I'm going to look at myself out there," Lettie said.

She walked toward the full-length, three-way mirror. Her face was flushed from the changing and wisps of hair were out of place, but still she looked at herself and knew she looked right. And looking right, she almost *felt* right. She lifted onto her toes, feeling for once delicate, light, and practiced.

ON the day she was discharged, Amber's parents arrived before group but she insisted on joining the circle one last time. The therapeutic conch made its way around. If you dug just a little bit, the sand beneath was cool, so Lettie shoved her fists in her pockets. One boy shared his memory of a man who wore a sweat-stained baseball hat. Another talked through an overwhelming fear of swimming in murky pond water. A girl who always cried, cried again for her two brothers, both killed in a freak fire, an accident that she felt responsible for because she'd left a scented candle burning on a shallow ledge. Amber followed the conch with her eyes until it was hers. Then she rested the shell on her knee and told how her boyfriend's skin turned gray when the leukemia got bad, the color of a sea slug, and how his tongue and ankles became so swollen he could not eat; he could not walk. She said she kept fucking while he seemed to want to rest, and she hadn't forgiven herself yet.

Charles said, "Everyone is a little afraid to leave."

"I'm not afraid," she said. And Lettie could see that she wasn't lying. Amber wasn't afraid of anything. She never had been. She was born fearless. She struggled with the consequences of extreme courage. "I guess I'm just saying thanks. My parents, they don't get it. It was good to just talk."

"Your parents may not understand completely, but they do care," Charles said.

Lettie could see Amber's parents sitting at a picnic table on the hill overlooking the bay. Behind them a flag snapped. She remembered the father dusting the bureau and the mother's trembling knees.

The girls exchanged addresses.

"I'm your first friend," Amber said. "But you're going to have lots of friends, Lettie." She zipped her bag shut and slung it over her shoulder. "Nothing could screw you up. Inside of you is all good. I was wrong about that, what I said before about you being a mess for life. Forget about the past."

Lettie thanked her, but didn't see her out or watch her meet her parents in the lobby. She didn't follow the car leaving. She opened her book, and read about the three children and their crystal ball. Within hours, two new girls were admitted. Each one with fresh hospital bracelets and greasy bangs.

Later that night when Lettie slid out of the window she wondered if her new roommates would tattle now that the equation was different, now that Amber was gone. She wondered, but it didn't matter. She'd been thinking more and more about Prem, what they'd done together, what else they might have done together had Amber not come along. Sometimes, on hikes with group, Lettie would pass a strong blossoming scent that came close to her memory of his, but still she hadn't found the exact match.

She followed the same route to Anthony's apartment, imagining the day she, too, would leave Randolph, unwilling this time to leave behind something she cared about. Anthony was a soft hulk on the easy chair, balancing a remote control on his knee, eating crackers from a stainless steel bowl. She knew she might regret knocking, but she knocked anyway.

Anthony didn't look surprised to see her, as if visitors in the night were commonplace.

"What can I do for you, Dolly?"

"I'm looking for Prem."

"Dolly, you want to know where Prem lives?"

"My name is Lettie."

"You look like a dolly to me. Like a doll baby. You know, his mama might not be happy if you rang her doorbell this late. Her head's always half off."

"Can you just tell him I was looking for him?"

Anthony pretended to jot a note on his open palm. "Dolly. Wants. A cripple." He smiled. "For sex. Is that it?" Lettie realized he'd been drinking. The realization came, and then so did, quickly, the yeasty scent.

He had said something so dreadful and true, so shameful she almost couldn't find the breath or the words to summon up a lie. So, instead, she'd said what she'd heard another girl say. "*Shut up. Screw you.*" And stalked off into the night.

As she turned onto the road, she saw Anthony switch off the TV. She knew she wasn't the first girl to tell him to screw off, but it still felt good to see him let down his blinds. First she followed the familiar road, then a less familiar road, until finally she decided to take a path she did not know, something that felt new, like progress. She came to the beach and walked with her sandals in her hands. Along the darkness the tide shushed over the rocky white shore, but out on the black horizon soft freckles of light indicated quiet vessels, each of them messaging: *Me, Me, Me.*

DISTRICT Court. *Family* Court. Outside, a confident brick one-story, its entrance balanced by two white columns, a symbol of fair-mindedness. Red geraniums dug in to cedar chips, both so sickeningly aromatic Lettie nearly retched. Deb paused on the steps to adjust her bangles. Within the building, a simple maze of mud-damaged green carpet, modern wood-paneled walls decorated with fire extinguishers, water fountains, a vending machine, a public telephone. Deb said, "Wait." And Lettie sat on a slippery leather bench, pulling her wide pink skirt as close to her knees as it stretched, waiting for her parents, *whoever they were*, to materialize.

EPILOGUE

WHAT IS IT about a place without people?

There are places people have vacated. It is said that if you take the hiking tour to the ghost town where Lettie lived, you can even now find family artifacts. A teddy in a ripped gingham jumper still resting on a child-sized bed, his ears rubbed clean of fur. Images of family life as it was. Other homes were routinely burned so that a couple of decades later the cellar hole in the woods seems unexpected, the cobblestone foundation a haunting surprise.

There are places where civilization has retreated. No water goes to these places. No electricity. No knowledge. Then there are extreme places where no one would choose to be. Places where the sound of your own voice is both too quiet and too loud. In your mind it is noisy, piteous, but it is subdued by the immensity of the woods. It comes out like your shriek during a paralyzed dream state. It is nothing, just nothing. There are sad places. Colorful places. Quiet places and loud. There are places you feel ill at ease. Places you forget yourself. In most of these places the future and the past are equally worthless. Serene places. Dead places. Places where animals with beaks and claws climb over downed tree trunks, where salamanders come up from the rot and wipe their noses. A place without people is still a place without people if one other person is there with you because over time you two become the same lost person.

No one belongs in a place without people. The standard definition does not include them. The law somehow abides to that. So Frank was sentenced to five years in a minimum-security prison, an orderly and clean, if aging, facility. He did not harm his daughter. He kept her. And for that reason, he was sentenced to the place where the gray linoleum peeled at the edges. The yellow doorframe paint chipped and showed the naked metal beneath. You could smell something like ripped cardboard, something like ripped coarse fiber. Frank sat at a table in the lounge, reading the newspaper. With what she knew, she had to laugh. He was reading *the newspaper*, as if current events mattered to him, as if they would any time soon. Deb and the prison attendant sat beside each other in front of the television and Frank stood as Lettie situated herself across from him.

His defender had done the talking in court. So had Lettie's. They had been onlookers of their own lives.

Frank's suit did not fit properly. On one side of Lettie Deb tisked, whispering, "I told the tailor to take in those underarms." On her other side, Lynn was partially sober except for two nips she cracked and swallowed on the drive. To Lettie she said, "I thought he would look older, older than this. I thought he'd be wizardly, if you know what I mean." She pressed her bleach-burned hands against her thighs to steady the withdrawals. That night in the lot outside The Randolph School Deb had shook her head and apologized into the steering wheel.

"What are you sorry for?" Lettie asked.

"Just this crying," was all she said.

One thing Lettie didn't know was that when she graduated from the program, they would give her a conch, identical to the one used in group. The gift made her realize that the shell was store-bought, in bulk, not something natural to the peninsula, not to the coast. She put hers on the bedstand in her new room at Deb's home, waiting for the final lesson to be revealed, for the concluding metaphor to crystallize.

She was enrolled in the public school. Lockers were assigned alphabetically. Hers was next to a boy's named Ben. Whenever they lined up, she stood next to this boy. On her first day, he asked where she'd come from. "Don't think you've ever heard of it," she said. Ben called her "Next in Line" and rubbed her shoulders, saying, "Loosen up, Next in Line. Loosen up."

Deb visited Frank on Thursday evenings and on Sunday mornings. Typically Lettie watched TV during this time. When she was home, Deb criticized Lettie for flipping channels. When she was gone, Lettie flipped and flipped until her eyes began to wear. One Saturday night, after Deb fell asleep, Lettie landed on a movie about a sick father. The mother and two daughters going about their cooking and washing, their tending, hearts leaking until the day the father died.

The next morning she and her grandmother emptied their pockets and placed their bags on the X-ray machine conveyor belt. Lettie passed through the scanner with no problem, but Deb set it off, bringing a heavy man with a wand to his feet. "It's my belt. I forgot to take it off," she said, loosening the buckle. "Your father is very ashamed of himself," Deb said. "He isn't himself."

Through the wired glass window, Lettie saw Frank in his orange uniform, sitting on the bench reading the newspaper. On either side of him, other inmates visited with their own guests. When the door opened, he stood. He smiled. And though Lettie felt awkward doing so, she smiled too.

"I didn't think you'd come," he said.

"I almost didn't."

"I wouldn't have blamed you."

When silence starts between two people, it grows. It grows like a bacteria, both because it is invisible and because it is fast-moving. Lies not included, Frank and Lettie had many years of feverish silence to rise above.

"I wanted to spare you," Frank admitted.

"Spare me?"

"I wanted to spare you."

Danceland was so pleasing, the very idea of it. Though they lived in its crumbling remains, with his stories, Frank had made it alive for Lettie. Sometimes, even now, she dreams of it vividly. Her mum, Lynn, lighting a tiki torch in the yard, unfolding chairs for a lawn party. Amber and her dead boyfriend having a petty disagreement by the porch door and laughing it off. Nosey in her arms. Caroline Brody Taylor somersaulting, walking on her hands, dancing. Prem telling Frank a story, making him laugh so hard he slaps his knee to relieve some of the force of all of that happiness. In Lettie's dream there are no airplanes buzzing overhead. They are all content to be where they are. In the evenings, lightning bugs dance on everyone's shoulders and knees.

Frank talked about prison food: slop served on Styrofoam plates, plastic forks, carried on melamine trays the color of butter. "You can cook," he said, remembering what Lettie would do with their once-a-week steak or chicken.

"I can handle it," Lettie said. "Whatever it was. I could have handled it."

"I don't agree," he said. "I'm relieved. I'm proud. I'm sorry. But you have to know, I'd have spared you this. You'd have never known."

"You should have told me."

"I hold back. If I hold back, it's because I'm protecting you."

Lettie asked about Carolyn, about her health, just as someone would ask about a distant aunt, connected to them, but not by much. Frank said that she found it harder and harder to travel. She couldn't navigate getting her luggage from point A to point B. Lettie said she understood, completely, how impossible it would be for her to come here, under any circumstance.

The mealtime buzzer rang at quarter to noon. Frank licked his lips despite himself. It was hard to see his eyes beneath the thick and flyaway eyebrows, the heavy defensive forehead. What Lettie could usually see, when he looked at her directly, was apology. This time, when he checked with her before their goodbye, she noticed in the reduced color, in the various tightness and slackness of his skin, the complexity of her father's true intention. He was sorry. He had wanted to spare her. He was sorry he hadn't spared her. But he was relieved. He was relieved that his work was done, even if he'd failed.

Deb respected their privacy, up to a point. She left them alone, but once in the car, her questions came one after another. What was said? How was it said? Months prior, Lettie might not have told her. She'd have kept it private, as a conversation between two people is likely to stay when there are only two. But she and Frank weren't just two to her anymore. They were . . . complicated.

Deb's apartment was situated halfway to town, halfway to the harbor. Later that evening Lettie walked to the water, where she often found her mother. Tufts of late-summer weeds, hardy and tall, grew from the cracks in the sidewalk and from between the concrete walkways of Deb's neighbors. Part of Lettie wanted to pull them all up, clean the unsightly mess. Then the street intersected with Shore Drive and it was time to cross toward the water.

A boat launch and restaurant decorated the pier. On Fridays and Saturdays, there was a band and an outdoor bar on the patio. Lettie sat on one of the massive limestone benches that lined the gravel path. Lynn often sat there too, arm in arm with some sunburnt man, the two of them oversexed and boozy. Whenever the man would amble to the liquor store on the Drive, its neon-orange sign flickering, Lynn would link her arm with her daughter's. That was the thing. Lynn's arm needed to be linked. Her mum needed to be tethered somehow to someone at all times. Just as Lettie did, in her core.

At sunset, the water turned dark before it turned white, before the moon rose to prominence and the shelter re-opened its doors.

"Are you breathing hard?" she asked.

"I don't think so," Lettie said.

"Don't be so nervous all the time."

"I guess it's getting a little cold. I might be shivering."

The wind had picked up and whipped the rigging of the docked boats. To Lettie, the clanging and snapping seemed coordinated, set to a tune. As if in that thrashing there was a beat, a subtle pulse. Lettie was always so eager to hear music.

Sincerest thanks to my family. I owe it all to my mother and father for filling my childhood with books and offering me the time to read them. To Cindy Burke for the long talks and, of course, the medical advice.To Kim Chinquee for being there word by word. To Myfanwy Collins for her sensitive advice. To my dear Hot Panthers: Mary Akers, Randall Brown, Lydia Copeland, Pia Z. Ehrhardt, Utahna Faith, Avital Gad-Cykman, Scott Garson, Tiff Holland, Liesl Jobson, Jeff Landon, Mary Miller, Darlin' Neal, Ethel Rohan, Jim Ruland, Gail Siegel, Claudia Smith Chen, Carrie Hoffman Spell, Girija Tropp, and Joan Wilking. To Mark Cote for pointing me to the snapshots of children taped above the beds in the women's dorm. To Kathy Fish for publishing an excerpt in *Necessary Fiction* and Gabe Durham for publishing a portion in *Dark Sky Magazine*. To Erin Knowles McKnight for her faithfulness to this book even when I was wrong, late, and/or stubborn. And to my husband Adam for everything else.

JENNIFER PIERONI grew up in a small, rural town in central Massachusetts, studied writing at Emerson College in Boston, and now lives on the north shore of the state with her husband and son. Her fiction has appeared in numerous literary journals and anthologies, including *Guernica*, *Wigleaf*, and *PANK*. She served for more than a decade as the founding editor of *Quick Fiction* and currently works as a grant writer in the nonprofit sector.

CPSIA information can be obtained at www.ICGtesting.com
Printed in the USA
BVOW04*1936180214

344993BV00001BB/1/P

9 781938 466205